A NOVEL BASED ON THE LIFE OF

FATHER EUSEBIO KINO

DESERT
MISSIONARY

Nicole Gregory

THE
MENTORIS
PROJECT

Desert Missionary is a work of fiction. Some incidents, dialogue, and characters are products of the author's imagination and are not to be construed as real. Where real-life historical figures appear, the situations, incidents, and dialogue concerning those persons are based on or inspired by actual events. In all other respects, any resemblance to actual persons, living or dead, events, or locales is entirely coincidental.

Mentoris Project
745 Sierra Madre Blvd.
San Marino, CA 91108

More information at www.mentorisproject.org

ISBN: 978-1-947431-41-6

Library of Congress Control Number: 2021949528

All net proceeds from the sale of this book will be donated to Mentoris Project whose mission is to support educational initiatives that foster an appreciation of history and culture to encourage and inspire young people to create a stronger future.

The Mentoris Project is a series of novels and biographies about the lives of great men and women who have changed history through their contributions as scientists, inventors, explorers, thinkers, and creators. The Barbera Foundation sponsors this series in the hope that, like a mentor, each book will inspire the reader to discover how she or he can make a positive contribution to society.

Contents

Foreword

First and foremost, Mentor was a person. We tend to think of the word *mentor* as a noun (a mentor) or a verb (to mentor), but there is a very human dimension embedded in the term. Mentor appears in Homer's *Odyssey* as the old friend entrusted to care for Odysseus's household and his son Telemachus during the Trojan War. When years pass and Telemachus sets out to search for his missing father, the goddess Athena assumes the form of Mentor to accompany him. The human being welcomes a human form for counsel. From its very origins, becoming a mentor is a transcendent act; it carries with it something of the holy.

The Mentoris Project sets out on an Athena-like mission: We hope the books that form this series will be an inspiration to all those who are seekers, to those of the twenty-first century who are on their own odysseys, trying to find enduring principles that will guide them to a spiritual home. The stories that comprise the series are all deeply human. These books dramatize the lives of great men and women whose stories bridge the ancient and the modern, taking many forms, just as Athena did, but always holding up a light for those living today.

Whether in novel form or traditional biography, these

books plumb the individual characters of our heroes' journeys. The power of storytelling has always been to envelop the reader in a vivid and continuous dream, and to forge a link with the subject. Our goal is for that link to guide the reader home with a new inspiration.

What is a mentor? A guide, a moral compass, an inspiration. A friend who points you toward true north. We hope that the Mentoris Project will become that friend, and it will help us all transcend our daily lives with something that can only be called holy.

—Robert J. Barbera, Founder, The Mentoris Project
—Ken LaZebnik, Founding Editor, The Mentoris Project

Chapter One

CURIOUS BOY

Martino Martini trudged up the steep, grassy mountainside and breathed in the warm, fragrant air that wafted from the fields of yellow wildflowers. He stopped to look around. How good it was to finally be back in the Italian Alps after traveling through China for so many years! His legs were sore, the sun was setting, and he was very, very hungry.

A handsome man with an unkempt beard, the twenty-nine-year-old Jesuit missionary was tired but would not let himself slow down—he was getting close to the village of a distant cousin.

He carried his belongings on his back; among them were treasures that he guarded carefully. He was out of breath but determined to go on. It was 1653, and he longed to tell Rome stories of what he'd seen as a missionary in China. Happily, his cousin's village, where he hoped he would be given food and a place to sleep, was on this route.

The familiar scenes—sharp mountaintops, crystal-clear lakes, and medieval castles poking up from tree-covered hillsides—elated and comforted him. Hearing Italian and German, languages he understood, picking berries from bushes just like when he was a child, and eating food with familiar flavor offered by kind peasants along the way—these God-given joys buoyed his spirits.

At last, he entered Val di Non, a fertile valley of lakes and mountains dotted with crooked old apple trees. The late afternoon light cast a golden glow against the next hilltop, where he spotted his destination: the village of Segno, where his cousins Margarita Chino and her husband, Francisco, lived with their young son, Eusebio.

Martino quickened his pace—there they were! Their figures were bent over and working the field next to their sturdy stone house. It had a steep timber roof, built so winter snow would easily slide off. The home was surrounded by tall pine trees that rustled in the summer breeze.

"*Buongiorno!*" he shouted, breaking into a sprint as Francisco turned toward him. "It is me, Martino!" His cousins dropped their tools and rushed toward him with broad smiles and open arms.

"Martino, what a pleasure! Where have you come from?" Margarita said, embracing her cousin for the first time in years. She noticed his Jesuit robe was dirty and tattered. Yes, it was her dear Martino, but he appeared gaunt now.

"I have been in China, yes, very far away, but I knew I wanted to return here."

"*Benvenuto, entra, entra!* Eat dinner, stay with us, and rest," Francisco said, throwing an arm around Martino's shoulder. "You look like you could use a good meal."

"Indeed, you are right," Martino laughed with relief.

Watching from the doorway of their stone cottage was eight-year-old Eusebio, Francisco and Margarita's only son. As his parents and Martino reached the house, Eusebio ran out and stared up at this stranger.

"Hello, I am happy to meet you," Martino said, reaching down to shake Eusebio's hand. "When I last saw you, you were just a baby." Wide-eyed, Eusebio shook the man's hand. Over dinner of cooked rabbit and warm bread, Francisco told Martino the news of their family since he'd been gone.

"We've had too many years of senseless fighting. Young men in our region became mercenaries," Francisco said, shaking his head, "to fight for whichever side will pay them. And when these men don't get paid, they plunder villages and take what they can from the farms. Peace, that is all we want. With peace, we have a chance to live as God wishes us to live."

Eusebio listened to his father, taking in every word, his eyes shifting from one adult to another. Both his parents were expressive, with open smiles and friendly gestures.

"Martino, enough of this—tell us about your adventures in China," Margarita said.

"Ah, so much to tell!" Martino said. "There is a great river called Yangtze, with boats so big that entire families live on them. The Chinese have made many canals so farmers can easily bring their goods to cities along the waterways."

3

"Do they have a king?" Eusebio blurted.

"No, but they do have an emperor," Martino replied. "He lives in a palace called the Forbidden City with many gardens, rooms, and courtyards."

Eusebio's shyness suddenly evaporated and questions tumbled out, his imagination working fast. "Did you have to cross an ocean to get there? How did you find your way?"

"I crossed several oceans on big ships," Martino said. Noting young Eusebio's intense curiosity, he added, "I drew maps of the lands over which I traveled in China. I intend to take them to Antwerp to be printed. Would you like to see them?"

Eusebio vigorously nodded his head as his parents smiled and cleared the table. Martino carefully opened his bag, took out several rolls of thick parchment, and unfolded them across the tabletop so all could see. Eusebio's eyes widened. Martino had drawn a detailed map with pictures and notes along the edges that explained the characteristics of each region of land and water. In Latin and Mandarin, he'd written the names of villages and towns, and notated the distances between them.

The intricate maps mesmerized Eusebio. He followed the lines that indicated hills, rivers, and mountain peaks, wondering if those places looked like the beautiful landscapes of the Tyrol region of his home. He wondered, *Are there children in China just like me?*

"The people of China are mostly poor, but like us they are good farmers," Martino said. "They have all kinds of superstitions. But when I meet people who seem strange, I look into their eyes and I see they are human beings, just like me. I want to

4

tell them about our God, our Christianity, but first I learn how they live and what they do."

"When you were on the ship on the ocean, how did you know where to go?" Eusebio asked.

By now it was nighttime, and Martino replied with a question of his own. "Do you know how to find pictures in the stars, Eusebio?" The boy shook his head no. "Well, I used these constellations to guide me."

Martino took him outside and pointed to the North Star, then to the Great Bear and Little Bear constellations. He explained how sailors used specific stars and constellations to navigate across the vast ocean. Eusebio was so interested that, in the following days, Martino taught the boy rudiments of astronomy and even some mathematic calculations.

Eusebio shyly brought out his own maps of the hills surrounding their farm and village. He'd drawn them on long pieces of tree bark.

"Ah, Eusebio, I see you are a cartographer like me," Martino said. "Maps are very important in exploration. They help us understand where we are and how to find where we are going. With maps, everyone can understand the lands that lie beyond our little village."

After a restful week, Martino thanked the little family and prepared to leave for his journey to Antwerp. Eusebio ran to his cousin and spoke with earnestness. "When you go to China again, I want to go with you," he said.

Martino smiled and touched the boy's head. "You are a brave

boy, but you must be strong to travel great distances. Help your parents now and have faith—dreams come true by remembering them, working for them, and asking for God's help."

With tears welling up in Eusebio's eyes, he watched his cousin's figure disappear over the next hill. His parents looked at each other. Their young son had been inspired by Martino's adventures and his kindness. After Eusebio went to bed that night, they talked about him. They'd seen how excitedly he'd learned everything Martino taught him—he would eventually need more stimulation than the dull work of farming.

Meanwhile, Eusebio lay wide awake in his bed. He thought about Martino's words and tried to visualize the oceans and faraway countries with strange names—he could get there if he could see the pictures in the stars. Eusebio's mind reeled.

Finally, the boy became drowsy. Something had changed deep within his young soul. A map—yes, a map—had been given for his imagination. Now he knew where he was and where he wanted to go in his life. He wanted to be a real cartographer and traveler, like his cousin. He wanted to know how to read the stars and how to map exotic new lands.

In the following weeks and months, Eusebio became restless. "I know every tree there is to climb, Papa," he complained to his father. "I know every stream and every good rock to hide behind."

He had free rein to roam the countryside. He'd found a horse that a neighbor no longer wanted and rode it bareback over the fields, following trails along the edges of hillsides. He made friends with other children and brought them along on his horseback explorations.

His parents sent him to a nearby school, hoping it would fill his appetite for learning, but he quickly outgrew it. He was as bored as the lizards sunning on the hot rocks and as restless as the birds darting in the trees. He knew there had to be life beyond the farm's dreary routines. He watched his parents work until dark every weekday, just to be sure they had enough to eat.

When Eusebio turned twelve, his parents sent him to a Jesuit school in nearby Trento. He took to the rigorous studies like a fish to water. The Jesuit priests, who were educated and disciplined, but also courageous, fascinated him. On his sixteenth birthday, he begged his parents to send him to the Jesuit College in Innsbruck, Germany. They agreed, but with deep sadness. They watched as he left their little village, turning to wave as he climbed the last hill that would take him north.

"Your name?" asked an elderly Jesuit priest, seated at a large wooden desk in the great hall of the Jesuit College of Innsbruck. A shaft of sunlight fell on the paper he wrote, making it blaze white. The man had wispy white hair and light blue eyes, and he held a long quill pen as he looked expectantly at the young man before him. It was a humid day in late August—the day all new students came to register at the university.

"Eusebio Chino," the young man said proudly. He was of a stocky build with thick, wavy brown hair and lively dark eyes. His smile was wide and playful as he looked at the seated priest.

He was eager to begin his new life here with the Jesuits, who were known for their great knowledge, belief in education, and courageous missionary work in far-off lands. Eusebio was ready to be part of it.

"Year of birth?" the man asked.

"1645," Eusebio answered. "I am seventeen years of age."

"You're Italian?"

"I am from Trento in Tyrol," Eusebio blurted. "But I hesitate to say whether I am Italian or German, for the city of Trento uses the language, customs, and laws of Italy almost entirely, and although it is located on the very edge of Tyrol, nevertheless, Tyrol is under the rule of Germany."

"Parents?" the man asked tiredly, hoping this answer would be short.

"Francisco and Margarita Chino," Eusebio said.

An unexpected wave of sadness flooded the young man's heart. Yes, he wanted a new life here with the Jesuits, but he missed his parents. When would he see them again? They had watched over him for years.

"Take your belongings to your room," the old man said gruffly, startling Eusebio out of his reverie.

"Thank you, Father—?" Eusebio asked.

"Father Antonio Rocca," the man said, waving him away.

Eusebio quickly picked up the meager items he'd brought from home—some clothing, a map, and his treasured sling-shot—and took them to his new room. He sat on the narrow, hard bed and placed his belongings on the one small table. Then he rushed out to explore the school and all its buildings.

Though it was late summer, the air was already cool. Peeking into the classrooms, Eusebio marveled at globes and at maps affixed to the walls. And books—he could not wait to open them! The other students were boys his own age, and he immediately knew he would find good friends here.

The Jesuit school's classrooms, built in heavy stone, were chilly. Their sturdy, old wooden chairs were uncomfortable; some had splinters. The teachers, mostly young men in their twenties, were strict and set high standards for their young pupils.

But Eusebio shrugged off the difficulties, a characteristic noted by his teachers. He was cheerful, energetic, and extraordinarily focused for a teenager. He had a certain wild streak of a boy who'd experienced freedom from an early age, which gave him brash confidence. Yet he listened intently to each lesson, grasped the particulars quickly, and worked almost obsessively until he found the answers to complex problems. In geography classes, he relished the sight of maps presented by his teacher and memorized the names of countries, mountains, and oceans.

Then, just as autumn turned to winter and the trees' golden leaves fell on the campus grounds, Eusebio visited the city of Hala in the Tyrol to see two childhood friends.

On the way, he began feeling strangely weak. He normally had great stamina, such that he took his good health for granted. But as he approached Hala, he struggled to walk without stumbling. His friends greeted him with alarm, immediately seeing that he was ill. They insisted he lie down to rest. But even after Eusebio had slept for many hours, he awoke fatigued, with sweat dripping down his face and neck. His heart raced, though he barely moved. Walking became painful, and soon he could not get out of bed. A doctor from Hala came to see him, but could not diagnose his illness.

Eusebio felt darkness closing in. He awoke in the bed, agitated and frightened. Was it day or night? Was he alive or dead? Was he at home or at school? Life was slipping out of him.

In his confused and nearly delirious state, he prayed desperately. "With the help of Saint Francis Xavier, O God, heal me from this sickness. If I recover, I promise to dedicate my life to the missionary work that he began."

He fell back into the damp sheets and into a deep sleep.

Chapter Two

THE PROMISE

The doctor called it a miracle. Never had he seen a man so close to death recover so completely.

Within days of Eusebio's prayer to Saint Francis, he was able to sit up in bed and eat. Soon after that, he could walk unaided. His friends cheered when he announced he must return to the university as quickly as possible. They happily sent him off, relieved that what seemed like a dire illness had passed.

On his way back, Eusebio was somber. Since he was a boy, he'd had the faith in God that his parents had given him, but now he struggled to comprehend the apparent fact that his prayer had been heard. No one else knew about his prayer. He could easily continue his studies to become a mathematician and geographer, and no one could blame him for not carrying through with his promise to become a missionary.

As soon as he returned, he sought out Father Antonio

Rocca, who had greeted him on his arrival to the school. When he knocked on the Jesuit's office door, Eusebio was immediately invited in by Father Rocca's gravelly voice.

"What is it, Eusebio? You look well! I heard the news that you were deathly ill." The old man shook his head with a smile and gestured for Eusebio to sit in a heavy wooden chair next to his desk.

"Father, I want to tell you something," Eusebio said hesitantly as he sat down. "When I was ill, I had many dreams. And when I was most sick—indeed, I felt death's grip closing over my heart—I prayed to God in the name of Saint Francis Xavier to be healed." Eusebio paused. "And I made a promise that if I were to recover, I would become a missionary, just as Saint Francis did, in his honor. And now . . ."

"Now you understand what your recovery means, am I correct?" Father Rocca asked.

"Yes."

"My son, you have been blessed with health. You have been given life for a reason. We are told to pray for God's will for us, which has now been shown to you. Indeed, the path may not be what you planned, but you must honor this blessing."

"I understand, Father. Thank you," Eusebio said, bowing his head. "Now my prayer will be for courage to follow God's will for me. The first step . . . is to enter the Society of Jesus."

Father Rocca smiled and did not speak. He was witnessing a rare transformation and he wanted it to unfold naturally.

"I want to be a Jesuit priest, like you, and a missionary, like Saint Francis."

"Very well. You may begin your novitiate immediately," Father Rocca said. "This is the right path for you, my son. I know it."

As Eusebio walked back to his room, he pulled his shoulders back to stand tall. It was 1665 and he was twenty years old. Yet he felt that in just a matter of weeks, he had grown into a man. Francis Xavier was now his own personal patron saint, the one in whose name his life had been saved. Eusebio decided then that he would honor this event by taking on his name. From now on, he would be known as Eusebio Francisco Chino.

His life's true purpose had been revealed: to become a priest and save souls throughout the world, wherever Rome may send him.

But first he had to undergo several years of training, which included long periods of silence, meditation, menial work, and prayer, in addition to academic studies.

Because all Jesuit priests were required to work as teachers, their studies were wide-ranging and rigorous. Eusebio gravitated toward philosophy, geography, mathematics, and astronomy. Even after his scholastic studies and novitiate requirements were over, his thirst for knowledge was not satisfied. He left the college and journeyed more than 250 miles away to the German city of Ingolstadt.

The University of Ingolstadt famously attracted the best scholars and thinkers in the world, and thousands of students enrolled. Eusebio hoped he might continue his studies there, and possibly teach.

He was eager to study advanced mathematics and geography, but he was excited to explore Ingolstadt's lively streets too. He marveled at the great Danube River, the second-longest river in all of Europe. As he strolled along the water, he imagined all the different countries through which this river traveled. He wandered through alleys, peeking into courtyards, admiring the massive brick Cathedral of Our Lady and the tall ducal castle, and sampling foods sold by street vendors. This vibrant city life thrilled him. It was so different from his home village, where little happened or changed, year in and year out.

But he dedicated most of his waking hours to studying late into the evening. Eusebio burned many candles at his table, challenging himself by tackling the most complex problems first and not sleeping until he had solved them. Though he dreamed of missionary work, his academic studies nourished him.

Years passed pleasantly for Eusebio at the university, where he assisted the professors as often as he could. Among his teachers was the famous geographer Father Heinrich Scherer who appreciated the young man's intensity. After taking several classes with Father Scherer, Eusebio considered the older scholar a friend. The two ate meals together, talking about the boundaries of the known world and about how maps could best serve the exploration of uncharted lands.

One evening, as they strolled next to the Danube, Eusebio told Father Scherer what he remembered of his cousin Martino Martini's visit years before and of his colorful maps of China. He held out his arms wide to demonstrate the maps' size.

"I know of your cousin," Father Scherer said, nodding thoughtfully. "Those maps became well known once he convinced a printer to distribute copies. I have heard they contain great detail."

"Indeed, that is how I remember them," Eusebio said. "What I recall even more vividly are his adventures in China as a missionary. Most people he met had never seen a European before, and some were so frightened at the sight of him that they ran away! He learned to speak Mandarin and succeeded in converting many men to Christianity. He told me about the wide rivers and canals there, and an emperor who rules from a palace that is like a fortress."

"Missionaries are brave men," Father Scherer said.

"My cousin became like my own North Star," Eusebio said. "From his example, I saw the life I wanted to lead. Father, I . . . ever since I heard his stories of China, I have wanted to lead the life of a missionary, to follow in his footsteps to China. It is, after all, what Saint Francis did."

Father Scherer stopped walking and gaped at Eusebio. "But you are a scholar of mathematics and geography. Your future is here, my friend."

"I know. Yes, those subjects are important, and I love this university. But I made a personal promise to follow Saint Francis years ago, and somehow I must keep this promise. I am thirty years old now. I cannot wait forever."

The two men continued walking in silence. "Please keep an open mind," Father Scherer said. "You are a fine scholar. The essays and small maps you've been publishing in the journal are original and good. Your reputation is growing. Everyone sees you have a brilliant mind and a great deal of knowledge to impart to others. That is your gift. I think you would make a fine teacher—you would be an inspiration to the younger men."

Winters in Ingolstadt were snowy and cold. Eusebio and his fellow Jesuits Antonio Kerschbaumer and Adam Gerstle ran about in the snow, laughing and throwing snowballs.

"*Ich liebe den Schnee!*" Adam cried, forming a large snowball and aiming it at his friends.

Eusebio avoided the snowball by running toward the Jesuit residence hall, where he could warm himself in front of the roaring fireplace.

Spring was always welcome after the months of bitter cold. Students sat amongst the dogwood trees that bloomed with pink and white flowers. Rivers and streams swelled with melting snow. Summers were pleasantly warm, which meant everyone lingered outside long into the evening. And then autumn arrived once again, when rays of sunshine filtered through gold and red leaves throughout the city.

Eusebio could not bring himself to leave Ingolstadt. He continued to take on clerical research work at the university, and keep up his own scholarly research.

One day in 1676, a clamor arose outside the building where Eusebio studied. He rushed to the window and gasped as he peered out to the courtyard below. Ferdinand, the Duke of

Bavaria, stepped down from an ornate carriage followed by his old father, the Elector. The duke had long, dark hair and a white lace collar. Because he had invested much capital in the university, he felt duty-bound to periodically visit to inspect it.

Luckily, no one saw the distain in Eusebio's face as he drew away from the window. He hated pomp of any kind and was skeptical of authority figures. As far as he could tell, their sole purpose was to maintain dominance and control. Even though Ferdinand and his wife had proven to be different—they actually seemed to care about the lives of common people, and had insisted on the restoration of churches and monasteries damaged during the brutal Thirty Years' War—Eusebio was naturally suspicious.

Father Scherer was among the group with the duke, providing a tour of the university buildings. As soon as Eusebio returned to his desk, the door to the study room swung open and in walked the duke and his entourage. Father Scherer rushed forward to introduce the Duke of Bavaria and his father to Eusebio, who bowed deeply to the visitors.

"I am pleased to meet you at last. We have heard a great deal about your ability with mathematics and geography," the duke said, looking Eusebio in the eye, as if to determine for himself if this was true.

"I am humbled that this is your understanding, but many hardworking and inspired scholars have been drawn to this university, and I cannot claim to stand out," Eusebio said, glancing at Father Scherer and wondering what he had told the duke.

"We have heard this from too many men to make it a matter of mere favoritism," the duke said. "And this university should retain the best scholars in all of Europe. Therefore, I am offering you a professorial chair here."

Eusebio was dumbstruck. He had not been expecting the offer and struggled to find the correct response. "This—this is an honor too great for me," he stammered.

"Nonsense," the duke said. "From what I understand, this is well-deserved. Please let us know when you can begin."

Eusebio's mind worked fast. The offer was an honor, but what about his intention to become a missionary—was that to be forgotten? It couldn't be! But to refuse the Duke of Bavaria would be disastrous.

"I am sorry, but . . . I cannot accept," he blurted. "I am awaiting an assignment to go to China, to work as a missionary."

"I am disappointed, but I suppose the world will be better for it," the duke said after a long pause. "Father Scherer, could you please take us to the dining hall? I would like to see the new stained-glass windows." As they turned to depart, Father Scherer glanced sorrowfully at Eusebio.

Eusebio leaned heavily on his table once the men had left. Looking out at the trees, his stomach tightened into a knot. He did not like to disappoint these men.

Within a few months, he left for the city of Oettingen in Bavaria for his third probation, a kind of final test for Jesuit priests to once more declare their dedication. Of course, he passed—but to his dismay, it did not guarantee he would receive orders to travel. He returned without enthusiasm to Ingolstadt.

~

For years Eusebio had written to Father Giovanni Oliva, the eleventh Superior General of the Society of Jesus, seeking a missionary assignment. All six of his previous letters had gone unanswered, but he tried yet again.

"I feel so endowed with the spirit," he wrote, "that in any place or office whatsoever, even though it be most lowly, where I may be sent at the command of my superior, there I shall be most content." He hinted repeatedly that he was prepared to go to China. He watched as his friends received their assignments and left for foreign lands. The selection process was slow—Eusebio had no control over it.

He was continually restless, though he was hardly the only one. Many young men who entered the Society of Jesus carried the same burning desire within their hearts to follow in the footsteps of the brave Francis Xavier. Eusebio commiserated with his friends Antonio and Adam—they too wanted desperately to be assigned to Asia for missionary work, imagining themselves as heroes for God. Waiting for their chance was increasingly hard.

"Here we are, three able and faithful Jesuits, yet they do not assign us to a mission," Antonio said, shaking his head. The three young men were in the library, whispering loudly.

"I feel sure that Ignatius of Loyola and Francis Xavier would want us to do the work of converting heathens to Christianity, instead of staying here, where everyone is Christian," Eusebio said.

"Remember obedience, my friend," Antonio joked, slapping

Eusebio on his shoulder. This was a rule of the Society of Jesus that Eusebio found the hardest to accept.

Antonio and Adam rose to take their leave for the evening, but Eusebio remained in the library, one of his favorite places in the university. He turned to the book he'd opened that contained the writings of Saint Francis, and his eye fell to this paragraph:

> But let him to whom obedience has been entrusted and who is considered greater become as the lesser and the servant of the other brothers, and let him show and have the mercy toward each of his brothers that he would wish to be shown to himself if he were in the like situation. And let him not be angry with a brother on account of his offence, but let him advise him kindly and encourage him with all patience and humility.

Patience. Humility. Faith. Eusebio sighed. Yes, he would wait with humility, and have faith that his call would come.

Two weeks later, as he returned to the university after a walk along the Danube to clear his mind, he looked up to see his friends Antonio and Adam running toward him as fast as their cassocks would allow.

"Eusebio, we have a letter! Come and see!" Antonio said breathlessly. He opened the letter to read it aloud. It was from the Reverend Father Provincial of Upper Germany.

"Your Reverence shall send Father Antonius Kerschbaumer and Father Eusebio Chino; one should be sent for service in New Spain and the other in the Philippines, just as Your Reverence deems best or as it shall please them and as they shall choose for themselves."

The two men looked at each other and laughed. "So, he's leaving it up to us," Antonio said.

"You must choose first, Antonio," Eusebio said. His heart was pounding. The Philippines were so close to China—the land he had dreamed of for years. And yet, he could not insist for his wish over that of his friend.

"No, no, *you* must choose first," said Antonio, who also fervently wanted to travel to China.

Seeing that they both were sticking to positions of humility, Adam intervened. "All right," he said, "why don't we let God decide? Here, I will write the names of each place on two pieces of paper and fold them up. Then each of you shall pick one and that will be your destiny."

"A fine idea," Antonio agreed.

When this was done, each reached for a folded paper. Antonio's face lit up with delight—he picked the Philippines! Eusebio did his best hide his disappointment; he was horribly jealous. Antonio regarded his friend with embarrassment. He knew Eusebio ached.

Adam, watching the feelings of his two friends, said, "I too have been assigned to the Philippines . . ."

"Mexico—or New Spain, as it is called—I never imagined going there," Eusebio said, grappling to find the right tone. He did not want his friends to feel sorry for him, so he quickly walked away, heading for the garden of the Jesuit residence and back toward his room. He wanted to be alone.

Maybe Antonio or Adam will not like Asia and I could take one of their places, he thought. *Maybe they will find it too difficult, or maybe one of them will fall ill, and I will be called to Asia after all.*

Even as these ideas passed through his mind, he realized they were foolish. His destiny was New Spain.

God must have a purpose for me in New Spain. Perhaps it's that I keep on going west to China!

Chapter Three

THE JOURNEY BEGINS

It was a glorious spring in the year 1678 when eighteen Jesuits gathered in Ingolstadt to begin a journey over the Alps on their way to Genoa.

Eusebio had his orders and he was eager to go. From Genoa, he would sail across the Mediterranean Sea through the Strait of Gibraltar to the Spanish port city of Cádiz. A ship was to depart Cádiz for New Spain, and the Jesuits aimed to be on it. There, Antonio and Adam would await another ship to begin their voyage to the Philippines.

Now that his departure day had arrived, Eusebio was prepared. He was thirty-five and ready to leave Ingolstadt for his greatest adventure—to see the world. He felt ready for any challenge.

He and his fellow Jesuit travelers were in good spirits as they mounted horses laden with supplies and began their long trip. His company came from Germany, Italy, the Netherlands,

Bohemia, Austria, and Hungary, and each had waited years to embark on a missionary assignment. The views of great Italian valleys and rivers filled them with excitement, joy, and reverence for God's creation.

On June 12, the Jesuits arrived in Genoa. There, they separated into groups and boarded small boats that took them to ships anchored four miles off the coast. Eusebio and six others climbed aboard the ship that was heading to Cádiz, and within hours it set sail. Eusebio was ready for any hardship, but he was pleasantly surprised that his bed, though narrow, was comfortable and that the meals served were tasty and plentiful. The Jesuits agreed on a schedule of prayers and a weekly mass. These gatherings were sparsely attended during storms, but many came afterward to thank God for their survival.

Eusebio stayed on deck as much as possible. He was riveted by the open Mediterranean waters and observed how the colors of the sky and water changed hourly. At night, he stared up at the black sky filled with glittering stars and thought of his cousin Martino, the first Jesuit he'd ever known. He remembered how, long ago, Martino had shown him the North Star and traced for him the patterns of many constellations. Eusebio smiled at the memory; he longed to see Martino and his mother and father in Segno. Were they looking at the night sky at this moment too?

May God keep my family safe. May they know I think of them always, he prayed.

The next morning, Eusebio caught sight of land. "What are those peaks?" he asked one of the sailors.

"Those are the mountains of Corsica," the man said gruffly,

as if it were common knowledge. Eusebio gazed at the mountains majestically rising from the distant island. He wished he could explore them. Suddenly, his eye caught a dark form in the water near the ship.

"What's that?" he exclaimed.

"Ah, Father, nothing to fear," the sailor said with a laugh. "That's a whale. He is probably just curious about the ship. Don't forget—the sea is his home, not ours." Eusebio gasped as the whale surfaced, displaying the full length of his magnificent body, and spouted water ten feet up into the air.

From that day on, Eusebio spent hours scanning the ocean's surface, hoping to see another whale. As he lost himself in the ripples of dark gray water, he contemplated his future. This journey was sponsored by the Spanish, and though he was grateful for the opportunity, he knew well that missionary work in New Spain served the ambitions of Spanish rulers. Would they get in his way?

Some Spanish said the natives should be so grateful for the civilizing effects of Christian teachings that they should perform free labor on their plantations—an even trade. Eusebio did not see it that way, though he was careful to keep this opinion quiet.

This is exactly what makes the missionary work so difficult, he thought. Not surprisingly, the native people of New Spain considered the Spanish—and priests—not just untrustworthy, but dangerous.

"Ahoy! Vessels on the horizon! Alert the captain!" Shouts from a sailor high up in the crow's nest interrupted Eusebio's thoughts.

Suddenly, the deck was alive with sailors scrambling to prepare for attack. Pirates were common in these waters, and they spared no one. Eusebio was unsure what to do—he had no weapons and he hated violence of any kind. Were they going to perish before even reaching Spain?

After an hour, a call came from the crow's nest: "They're English ships—no cause for alarm!"

Sea wind whipping his face, Eusebio bowed his head to offer a prayer of thanks. That evening, more sailors than usual attended the Jesuits' prayer service and asked for confession. Eusebio realized how much these men feared an encounter with pirates.

Finally, after many weeks, the shores of Spain came into view. The ship approached the city of Alicante, where Eusebio spotted a lighthouse and a citadel on top of a mountain. The ship turned into the port and anchored in order to bring new supplies aboard. On shore, a group of Jesuits from Alicante invited Eusebio and the others to stay for several days. They politely accepted the invitation, but Eusebio worried, *Will this make us late for the ship from Cádiz to New Spain?* Ships sailed for New Spain about once every two years—missing this one would mean a long wait until the next.

To everyone's relief, they soon set sail again, traveling along Spain's southern coast toward the Strait of Gibraltar and on to Cádiz. The skies darkened and storms slowed their course. When the sky cleared, a fleet of unidentified ships again appeared in the distance, setting off panic among the crew and passengers. As the ships drew closer, they were identified as friendly Dutch merchants. Eusebio was relieved, but suddenly an argument erupted on the deck.

"You seem to have no plan for an actual attack," an elderly passenger snapped at the captain.

"Be glad this crew is able-bodied, strong, and dedicated to defending you and everyone else! Or maybe you'd prefer we give *you* a sword to kill a few pirates?" the captain retorted.

Eusebio intervened. "Captain, we are all grateful for your skills and for the strength of your sailors. The fear of pirates has everyone on edge," he said, glancing at the old passenger. "We all want to arrive in Cádiz safely."

The old man walked away without further words, but the captain turned to Eusebio with thanks. "I wish I had a peacemaker like you on every voyage," he said. "Quarrelsome passengers are all too common and can make relations stressful. Thank you for calming that old man."

Eusebio bowed slightly. "Of course, Captain."

Clouds darkened the clear skies once again, and the passengers awoke to find the ship enveloped in fog. The captain's navigators conferred and did not agree on the right course. Finally, the captain made the decision—and took the ship far in the wrong direction. By the time the fog lifted hours later and his mistake became known, they had lost a whole day. Once again, the journey was set back.

At long last, the harbor of Cádiz came into view, and Eusebio, whose face had become bronzed by the sun, spotted a fleet of ships in the distance. His stomach lurched. They were the Spanish ships, already sailing for New Spain.

He called out to the others, who ran to the rail to see for themselves. By the time they reached Cádiz, their fear was confirmed—they had missed the fleet that had just departed. It would be many months or years before the next ships would depart for New Spain. It took a long time to gather funds for such journeys, not to mention competent crews willing to risk their lives on the rough seas.

In God's time, Eusebio thought. He tried to console himself with prayer, but his disappointment ran deep.

The Jesuits' heavy mood lifted as they walked along the lively streets of Cádiz, an open city that jutted out into turquoise water with a comfortable climate and cool breezes. Its narrow streets opened up to views of the sea or of plazas with ancient monuments. It was a busy trading city, and Eusebio remembered this was the port from which Cristoforo Colombo had departed for his second voyage in 1493, heading to the West Indies.

The Jesuits decided to take up residence at a college in Seville, about seventy-five miles north. There, the Superior General gave them assignments. Fathers Gerstle and Kerschbaumer were told to assist in feeding the poor of the city, and others were ordered to minister to the sick. Eusebio was assigned to teach at the college, and he decided to make good use of this time to learn Spanish and study astronomy.

Whenever he could, he slipped out to explore Seville. He'd heard that an abundance of silver was flooding the merchants' stocks, brought back by Spanish explorers from New Spain. It was boosting the city's economy, and men who were newly wealthy could be seen strutting proudly on the streets in fine clothes.

But just as the city was finally recovering from the Great Plague a few decades before, the disease returned. It took lives from of every level of society, and Jesuits were among the many who died.

On one of his walks on a warm afternoon, Eusebio came upon a little girl lying in the doorway of a stone house. It was not uncommon to see orphans in the streets, but this child looked near death. He ran to her and kneeled down to touch her forehead. Her skin was pale and her dark hair was tangled and matted against her neck, but she had a pulse. Eusebio spoke to her and reached under her shoulders to lift her up just as he heard the sound of an approaching carriage.

"Stop! Padre, what are you doing?" a woman's sharp voice barked at him. He turned to see the door of the carriage fly open, and down stepped a fine lady in a dark, formal dress and jewel earrings. She was perhaps in her late forties, with smooth dark hair swept under a silk bonnet.

"This child is ill and must be taken to a doctor," Eusebio said with irritation. He did not rise, defying the customs of the time.

The woman stared. "Are you sure she is alive?"

"Yes," Eusebio replied, "but just barely. She needs help now."

"Bring her to my carriage. I know a doctor in this neighborhood who will help her."

The carriage driver moved to help lift the girl. As he did, he whispered in Eusebio's ear. "You are speaking to Duchess de

Aveiro, de Arcos, y Maqueda, wife of the Duke of Arcos—show respect!"

After the two men had safely placed the girl in the carriage, Eusebio bowed to the duchess. "Duchess, I am sorry. I am not from this place and did not recognize you. I am Father Eusebio Francisco Chino, a lowly Jesuit from the college here. Thank you for taking this girl."

"I am pleased to make your acquaintance," the duchess said. She contemplated his worn brown cassock and dark hair that curled over his ears. "I invite you to visit my palace tomorrow. I would like to know more about what you are doing here."

She turned and briskly climbed the carriage. The driver told Eusebio the address with a knowing smile and the carriage was off.

He didn't tell his Jesuit brothers where he was going. Eusebio exited a side door of the Jesuit college and found his way to the palace of the duchess—whose name, he'd learned, was Maria de Guadalupe.

He was shown in through the heavy carved wooden door and led by a servant to a lavishly furnished sitting room, where the duchess sat on a blue silk-covered chair. Since their encounter, Eusebio had learned she was a wealthy woman and a landowner, as well as an accomplished painter and linguist. Her faith was the foundation of her life, and she funded missions in many countries.

"So, you came. I am glad to see you," she said, smiling. She was more relaxed in her home, and Eusebio realized she was pretty. She had blue-green eyes, pale, delicate skin, and dainty silver earrings hanging from her ears. She was perhaps fifteen years older than he was. Eusebio blushed and looked down.

"I am glad to tell you the little girl is well," the duchess said. "She had not eaten in days. Her mother died a month ago, and she has not seen her father in years."

Eusebio looked up. "Thanks be to God that she is safe," he said.

The duchess began asking about the Jesuits. She knew little of their missionary work and was curious about Eusebio's life in Germany and his future in New Spain. She was surprisingly comfortable speaking with him; she was educated, curious, and did not seem to care about typical formalities—a kindred spirit! Eusebio was not used to being in a woman's presence, especially one as charming as the duchess. She explained that she had been born in Portugal but mostly lived in Madrid, and she once had a spiritual experience as a child.

"I was only a girl of ten when I—I encountered Jesus," she began shyly, not sure how Eusebio would react. He looked at her without a trace of doubt, waiting for her to explain. "I was just waking from an afternoon nap and I saw a candle flame on my desk. When I rose to go to it, the face of Jesus hovered within the flame. I was filled with joy—I felt that we under-stood each other. He was there for just a few minutes, then his face faded and it was just a candle again—but I was changed. I knew I'd had a vision, and I wanted to become a missionary nun. I begged my parents, but they would not allow it. So, I continued at school. But I have always followed the work of our missionaries—I admire their courage. And now I am able to help fund some missions, perhaps even yours."

"And the duke, your husband? Where is he now?" Eusebio asked, immediately regretting it. The duchess's pleasant demeanor vanished and she looked sad and angry all at once.

"I have divorced him," she said. Eusebio kept silent.

The duchess rose abruptly, signaling the visit was over. Eusebio jumped up and bowed deeply.

"I want to see you again," she said, taking Eusebio's hand. "And I want to know when you are departing. I may be in a position to fund your missionary work."

Eusebio bowed once again and left.

Two pleasant and fruitful years passed in Seville. Once he realized he would have to wait a long time for the next ship, Eusebio decided to use the time to become fluent in Spanish. His frequent visits to the duchess were filled with friendly, stimulating conversation. Before long, he learned that the ship *Nazareno* was prepared to leave for New Spain, so he paid a last visit to the duchess.

"I am leaving on Friday, God willing," Eusebio told her. They were in her sitting room, as usual.

"Just think, in just a few months' time, you will be in another world, where you will see nothing familiar," she said. Eusebio heard the envy in her voice.

"I will write to you and describe it all," he said. He meant it. She had become the only person with whom he felt wholly comfortable sharing his innermost thoughts.

"I hope you do. I want to know everything you see. Had I more courage, I might have made missionary work my purpose. But I am glad you are going on this journey. I will pray every day that you are protected and guided, wherever your work takes you."

The two friends looked at each other in silence, each wondering if they'd ever see the other again. Then they rose to shake hands formally, and Eusebio left. The duchess hurried to her window and watched as he walked away down the cobblestone street.

With great excitement, the Jesuits returned to Cádiz and boarded the *Nazareno* on a cloudy day with a wind that made white caps rise up across the water.

As the *Nazareno* eased out of the harbor under gray skies, the wind turned blustery. Within an hour, a violent storm swept in, tossing the ship over mountainous waves. The ship's captain barely had time to turn the vessel around before it hit rocks, ripping a hole in its underside. Passengers shrieked in terror. Eusebio was thrown against a wall and could barely stand in the violent rocking. *Is this the end, before we even begin?* he wondered.

Miraculously, the *Nazareno* did not sink, and after the wind subsided, the captain maneuvered the damaged ship back to the harbor. Exasperated, the Jesuits were forced to return to Cádiz. That night, Eusebio wrote to the duchess:

While we were going out of the harbor, our vessel grounded on the cliffs in the most evident danger of the foundering with

*all on board. But by the favor of His Divine Majesty and the
intercession of Saint Francis Xavier, the sea became calm again
and we returned safe and sound to the city and to our college at
about eight o'clock in the evening.*

Eusebio knelt at the small altar of the Jesuit chapel to give
thanks for safety and to pray for patience. He restlessly slept in
one of the rooms at the back of the chapel, and awoke just before
dawn. Rising, he decided to walk along the shore to gaze at
the stars. The sand was smooth and cool as the waves quietly
washed in. Suddenly, a round, pearl-white light with a long tail
appeared in the lower night sky.

A comet! Eusebio watched in fascination as the bright light
rose and arced across the heavens. From a nearby street, one man
shouted, and then another, as the few people who were awake
leaned out of windows and pointed to the glowing light. After a
long couple minutes, it faded.

Eusebio sat down on a rock to absorb what he'd just witnessed. God's power and beauty filled him with awe and fear,
but this comet—so bright and sudden! He believed, as did many
people, that comets presaged misfortune, such as the death of a
notable person, or a natural disaster, such as a flood or drought.
He thought immediately of the Duchess de Aveiro and feared
for her life.

He walked back to the chapel to write down his observa-
tions of the comet, and he vowed to do so every night it was
visible. Then he wrote to the duchess describing the comet—had
she seen it too? He expressed his deep hope that the comet was

not a sign of misfortune for her or her family. Though he did not mention this in the letter, he worried the comet signaled a return of the Great Plague, this time taking even more innocent souls.

Every night thereafter, he and other Jesuits went out to the beach of Cádiz. For seven weeks, just before dawn, they were dazzled by the appearance of the brilliant, glowing comet. Eusebio was in awe—it was another sign of God's endless creativity and surprise.

But he was also a scientist, so he noted the comet's size, brightness, and movement. Every morning, he wrote down what he had seen and calculated its distance from earth. He wondered, *What causes a comet to appear and disappear, and what is it made of?*

At last, in January 1681, a flotilla of ships was ready to sail to New Spain. Eusebio, now a passenger on the *Aviso*, watched the newly appointed viceroy of New Spain, the Marques de la Laguna, board the ship. Two armed galleons led the flotilla out to sea. Citizens and military men lined the shores of Cádiz, waving banners and shouting, "*Adios! La velocidad de dios.*"

The human figures on shore became small, then indistinct, and the shoreline finally disappeared. Eusebio turned away and crossed himself. He was more than ready for the new adventure to begin, yet he would never forget the sweetness of his home land, his parents, his friends, and the duchess.

He made a decision. From now on, he would spell his last name as Kino. He wanted be sure it would be pronounced in the proper Italian way, even after he reached New Spain.

Chapter Four

MEXICO

"Let us toast to our new arrival, Padre Eusebio Francisco Kino! Astronomer, mapmaker, and missionary!" cheered Don Isidro Atondo y Antillón. The gruff and somewhat burly Spanish admiral stood at the end of a heavy wood table, among a dozen other men, including Eusebio. Servants placed plates of food and glasses of wine before the guests. Candlelight flickered across their faces.

"I'm pleased to tell you he has also been named vicar of this region," Atondo said.

The dinner guests raised their wine glasses, turning toward Eusebio with smiles and nods. The dining room in the cool stone hacienda had wide, open windows. The night air was fragrant with flowers from the surrounding gardens.

"Thank you," Eusebio responded with effort. He wanted to be gracious to his host, though he was uncomfortable among military men.

"Welcome to New Spain, Padre," Atondo said. "We have much work for you here. The native tribes are . . . unpredictable. But first, tell us about your voyage! Crossing the ocean is a dangerous adventure."

"Thank God that the captain was able, as our ship was battered by three strong storms," Eusebio said. "But even in good weather, the journey was difficult—rats ran freely on every deck, and the hard bunks and close quarters made sleep difficult. Our food, which tasted good at the beginning, eventually rotted, and the drinking water developed an unpleasant stink and taste."

The men at the table shook their heads, remembering their own difficult passages to New Spain.

"But God brought us safely here, and for this we are grateful," Eusebio continued. He explained how after his ship left the Canaries, it sailed across the Atlantic to Puerto Rico, then Santo Domingo and then Jamaica. They sailed along the southern coast of Cuba and stopped at several islands. From the Yucatán they crossed the Bay of Campeche.

"We reached Vera Cruz on May 9," Eusebio said. "Here I met the good Padre Matías Goñi from Spain. He has kindly agreed to work as my assistant." Eusebio gestured to the Jesuit priest sitting next to him, who smiled shyly. Padre Goñi was a small, quiet man with curly dark hair.

"And now that you've come down from the mountain into our city, what is your impression?" Atondo asked.

"It is a city of stark contrasts," Eusebio said warily. "Who could not admire the elegant cathedral and the splendid haciendas, with their gardens and fine ironwork? Yet the population is divided—the very wealthy and the very poor."

An uncomfortable silence followed Eusebio's words as the guests considered that the Jesuits probably judged them harshly for their wealth.

"Ah, but you will soon discern many other groups," Atondo said with a coarse laugh. "From Europeans, African slaves, and native tribes, we now have created mixed-blood populations."

"I have heard that in spite of the governor's laws, natives are used for hard labor with little or no payment," Eusebio said, looking the admiral in the eye.

"As long as you give them a cheap trinket, they are usually happy," said another guest, and everyone but Eusebio chuckled and nodded.

"Padre Kino, Padre Goñi, I assume you both know about last year's devastating attack north of here?" Atondo's dark eyebrows lowered and his expression turned grim.

"I do not know details," Eusebio replied. Padre Goñi shook his head *no*.

"I will let Don Antonio de Otermin explain," Atondo said, gesturing to the man on his right whose rough face bore two long scars. "He is the governor of New Mexico, and has honored us with a visit for several weeks."

All eyes turned to Don Antonio, who described what would much later become known as the Pueblo Revolt. "It was a long, bloody attack, Padre, precisely timed for the week when we were all low on supplies," Don Antonio said. "Nations of

Tanos, Pecos, Jemez, Queres, and others came together—their leader was a warrior named Popé. First they stole the horses and mules, so no alarm could be sent to other Spanish settlements. Then they invaded the settlements, targeting the Franciscan friars—they mutilated and killed nearly everyone."

"Why the friars?" Eusebio asked with a shudder.

"The friars had made it a practice to burn tribal religious items, destroy their ceremonial spaces, then humiliate and beat the spiritual leaders in the open, so all could see," Don Antonio explained.

All in the name of Christianity, thought Eusebio darkly.

"Before the attack began, I encountered a native I know well," Don Antonio said. "He carried two banners—one was white, for peace, and the other was red, for war. He said if the Spanish wanted peace, then they must leave the country immediately. If the Spanish choose the red banner, then we would perish.

"I tried to negotiate, but realized that the longer this took, the more time the tribes had to gather. Then I heard the terrible sound of war whoops echoing from the canyons, and I knew the attack was beginning. They swept down on us with guns and arrows. They were fierce and bold, setting fire to church doors and villas."

"How many men were part of the attack?" Eusebio asked.

"I would guess more than two thousand," Don Antonio said. "The rampage went on for nine days, despite the steadfast defense from our soldiers. We lost more than four hundred people—soldiers and colonists. I was wounded by an arrow to my face and a bullet to my chest, but I escaped with a small convoy of people. We had not a crust of bread, nor a grain of wheat or maize." He paused, then continued in a low, determined voice. "I will return next month to regain what we lost."

The dinner guests were silent. Eusebio wondered, *What bloody retaliation is he planning?*

"So, you see, Padre Kino," Atondo said, "this is our situation. The tribes must be subjugated by the military, but also by you. Your mission is to prevent uprisings. We conquer and you convert."

Eusebio nodded as a phrase from the Bible entered his mind. *"Blessed are the peacemakers, for they will be called children of God."* . . . *But you won't find them among the Spanish military,* he thought.

"May I change the subject?" asked a man from the end of the table. He appeared to be distinguished, though not a soldier. "Padre Kino, your reputation as an astronomer has reached even these shores. What were your impressions of the comet in January?"

"I observed the glowing comet from Cádiz," Eusebio said, pleased to dwell on a positive topic. "It was of great interest for many reasons—demonstrating God's power, being an apparent random phenomenon of the heavens, and also inspiring terror in many people."

"Padre, I introduce to you Don Carlos de Sigüenza y Góngora—a learned man like yourself, though no longer a

Jesuit," Atondo interrupted with a twinkle in his eye. Watching with interest, he tried to guess whether the two men would get along or disapprove of each other.

"I wrote a pamphlet about the comet's appearance," Don Carlos said to Eusebio with obvious pride, "and I would be delighted to share it with you. Its title is *Philosophical Manifesto against Comets Stripped of their Dominion over the Timid.*"

"Most intriguing! Indeed, I would like to read it," Eusebio said. *Perhaps this man can be a friend*, he thought, his hopes rising.

"I must warn you, Padre," Atondo said, "Don Carlos no longer takes a religious view of things."

Eusebio looked at Don Carlos curiously, as Atondo guided the conversation to the topic of Baja, an island to the west he hoped to explore. Spanish ships needed a safe port in Mexico on their way back from China, and Baja could be just the spot.

Walking back through the city streets after the dinner, Eusebio pondered all he had heard. Would he, like many other missionaries, become a martyr at the hands of the native tribes? He hurried back to his room to write to the duchess about the extraordinary dinner with the admiral and his guests.

One by one, Eusebio's Jesuit friends with whom he'd sailed to Mexico left to embark on missionary assignments to South America, the Philippines, and China. Each time a friend departed, Eusebio was awash in sadness for days. These friends had kept each other in good cheer during their long journey from Italy.

They had shared so much and now they realized they'd probably never see each other again.

Eusebio took his sadness to the rugged terrain of Mexico. He was eager to explore it, so he rode on horseback outside the City of Mexico, beyond the hot streets, past the elegant Spanish haciendas, and out into the stark, dry desert. He'd never seen such blazing, punishing sunlight, or breathed air so dry. He was fascinated by the flowering cacti, darting roadrunners, and rock-covered mountains.

He observed different groups of native people from afar and was embarrassed to see how little clothing the women wore. He averted his eyes, though the women displayed no sense of shame. In the desert, most often the native people kept to themselves. And when he walked anywhere near their settlements, Eusebio felt he was being watched.

In Mexico City, he was frustrated and tired of waiting for an official assignment that would give him purpose. He was eager to get into the hills as far as he could, to work and live among people to whom he could bring God. He longed to see where they lived, how they grew food. He wanted to learn their strange-sounding languages.

There was something else: The rocky mountains set against the deep blue skies triggered his boyhood eagerness for adventure. It was as if they spoke to him, *Come, climb each one. Come see what is on the other side.*

Don Carlos sent an invitation to visit. Eusebio washed his face and hands, brushed the dust from his boots and cassock, and set off for the learned man's home. He had been there several times since Atondo's dinner. In Don Carlos, Eusebio found an intellectual equal, and the two enjoyed lively discussions about astronomy and theology.

At his friend's modest estate, he was shown to a sitting room simply furnished with heavy, dark wood chairs and a small table set on a dark blue wool rug. Eusebio was surprised to see Don Carlos was not alone. An elegant young woman with dark eyes rose as Eusebio entered the room. By her clothing, Eusebio recognized that she was a nun, but her playful expression caught him off guard.

"Padre," she said in a low voice, her head bent slightly. "I have heard about you."

"Padre, this is Sor Juana Inés de la Cruz—not only a servant of God, but a witty poet and intellect. A gem in our midst," Don Carlos said with a smile.

"An honor to meet you," Eusebio said. He stared at her smooth brown skin and dark eyes. "Are you from Spain or . . . ?"

"I was born here, out of wedlock," she said, looking into his eyes as if to defy negative judgment. "My father was a Spanish captain and my mother was *criolla*, of Spanish descent. I was raised by my grandfather not far from here, in the shadow of two powerful volcanoes, Popocatépetl and Iztaccíhuatl. I seem to have gotten from them a certain fire."

Eusebio was at a loss for words in the presence of this clever young woman, but Don Carlos jumped in. "As a girl, Sor Juana worked as lady-in-waiting to the wife of our viceroy. With the help of the couple, she entered an intellectual contest of sorts. Theologians, philosophers, and poets challenged her with questions—Sor Juana answered them all correctly and with great poise. I was lucky to witness it."

"I wish I had been there," Eusebio said. "It is rare to meet a woman of such education and capability." As soon as these words left his mouth, Eusebio worried they were too forward. Sor Juana laughed.

"It's an old story—the men who hold positions of authority are blind to the talents and souls of people they consider beneath them. That includes women and the native people of this land. Those who have lived here long before the Spanish arrived are viewed as savages, to be used as slaves."

"Sor Juana won't tell you, but one of her poems is now famous. Please, Sister, give us just one stanza," Don Carlos said.

With pleasure, Sor Juana began reciting, "You foolish men who lay the guilt on women not seeing that you are the cause of the very thing you blame—"

Just then, a female servant brought in a tray with three small cups of tea and placed it on the table. Sensing that Sor Juana was about to talk about the repression of women in Mexico, Don Carlos steered the conversation in a different direction.

"Padre," he said, "I am eager to continue our talk about the comet."

"Of course!" Eusebio said. "Like everyone, I was astounded at its brightness and size. I could not estimate its distance from our land."

"I saw it too," Sor Juana said. "The comet was fascinating,

but so were the strong reactions to it from our people—they were attracted to the light and afraid of it at the same time."

Don Carlos shook his head. "I asked myself, is it a burning star? Is it a cloud of vapor in the heavens? Why did it last for several days? How far away was it? These questions still bother me!"

After their conversation fell silent for a moment, Eusebio changed the topic. "Don Carlos, I do not know why you are no longer a Jesuit, but you must realize that the greatest value of the comet's appearance is that people saw it as an omen from God. I do not want to argue with this view. When people lose the fear of God, they are more likely to sin with abandon, sometimes with violence."

Don Carlos's smile vanished. "Padre, are you implying that you want to use the comet to keep Christians in line? That's a false stance and you know it. You are a man of God, but also a scientist."

"My work as a scientist is to study God's many creations," countered Eusebio.

Sor Juana watched with amusement as the two men argued.

"Perhaps it is a coincidence that the appearance of comets throughout history have been followed by terrible events—floods and disease, as I'm sure you know," Eusebio said. "I simply believe the comet reminds us all of God's omnipotence and should make us humble."

"No! This is the very moment to elevate the common knowledge of the stars and sky, and our human place among them," Don Carlos said, exasperated. The two friends were irritated and disappointed in each other.

"Sor Juana, what is your view?" Eusebio asked.

"I believe you are both correct. While you may disagree, I hold both ideas to be true," she said.

Eusebio turned to his host. "My aim, Don Carlos, is to bring natives to an understanding of the Christian God. But I am also a practical man, and I hope to teach them skills so they can live prosperously."

Don Carlos looked away. This was exactly what he did not like about religious men—they put spiritual beliefs before all else. *And this priest wants to make natives prosperous? Ridiculous!* he thought. *The natives can never be equal to us—they simply do not have the mental capacity.*

Seeing that he'd upset his host, Eusebio rose from his chair. "I am afraid I must go. Don Carlos, I remain your friend and hope to see you again. Sor Juana, it was a pleasure to meet you."

Don Carlos forced a smile and shook Eusebio's hand. "Yes, yes . . . indeed." He watched the Jesuit priest leave his house with disdain, thinking, *He is learned and foolish all at once.*

When Eusebio returned to the Jesuit residence, he went immediately to his small room and stretched out on his bed, staring up at the high stone ceiling with heavy wooden rafters. He reviewed all parts of the stimulating evening. Sor Juana—a most unusual nun, and a poet! And Don Carlos, how angry he became when he discussed the comet. Eusebio decided to write a pamphlet of his own to clarify his understanding of the comet in religious terms. *I will start tomorrow*, he thought, made happy by this sudden goal.

He thought of his faraway friend, Duchess de Aveiro, her

face hovering above him. If only he could tell her all of this in person. *Those conversations we used to have in her sitting room . . . I miss them*, he thought while falling asleep.

Over the next two years, Eusebio attended many dinners and parties hosted by wealthy Spanish men—mostly military officers, but intellectuals too—and their wives in Mexico City. He was not impressed by wealth or status, but he was grateful to be part of the lively conversations and debates that took place at these social events. He was polite and outwardly good-natured, but he longed for his real work—his missionary work—to begin.

At last, word came from the viceroy—Eusebio and his assistant, Padre Goñi, were to sail from the west coast of Mexico to Baja California with Admiral Atondo. The region was strategically important: ships returning from the Philippines required a place to stop to replenish supplies—and Baja could be just the right location, but only if peaceful settlements could be established there so sailors could rest without threat. All previous attempts had been unsuccessful.

Eusebio and Atondo had by now developed a mutual respect, in spite of their differing viewpoints. The admiral was a skillful, confident leader, but he had little faith or piety, and he lacked compassion toward anyone he considered weak.

Eusebio's reputation as an intelligent Jesuit and a lively conversationalist was well known throughout Mexico City. His friendship with Don Carlos had cooled, but Eusebio's recently printed treatise on the comet had elevated his status in intellectual and royal circles. He sent several hundred copies to the duchess in Spain, asking her to forward them to friends there and in Italy.

He also sent a copy to Sor Juana. To thank him, she penned a sonnet praising his astronomical knowledge.

"Padre, you must ignore your many invitations to dinner and prepare for this journey," said Atondo, who insisted the priest meet with him at his home to discuss their trip to Baja. "We sail in three days."

Atondo opened two maps across his table so he and Eusebio could study their route. Eusebio's eyes lit up as he leaned over to the maps to examine them.

"We cross the Sea of Cortés here," the admiral said, pointing to the expanse of blue to the west of Mexico City. "The island of Baja is a desolate, rocky place, but pearl hunters have found the waters rich, especially in La Paz. The tribe called Guaycura lives there, a nomadic people who sometimes fight for territory rights with natives called Pericú.

"As you probably know," Don Atondo went on, "pearl hunting is dangerous, so other explorers from Spain made the mistake of enslaving Guaycura people and forcing them to do the work. Now the Guaycura keep their distance and do not trust us. Spanish settlements in Baja are small, but our viceroy, Marques de la Laguna, wishes to strengthen them. This means the Guaycura and the Pericú must find a way to live peacefully with us, under our control."

"Tell me, how many tribes are there in New Spain?" Eusebio asked. He had heard so many names of tribes that he was becoming confused. Before arriving in Mexico, he thought there might be two or three tribes, but there were far more.

Atondo looked at him, measuring how to introduce his friend to such a complex subject. "Do not make the mistake of thinking the tribes here are all alike," he said. "You will soon learn, Padre, that just as we have countries with unique languages, governments, leaders, and customs, so do the people here. Each region has many tribes. The Pima are skilled at farming the land. They have crops as abundant as any in Italy or Spain. And the Apaches—well, they have a reputation of aggressively trying to dominate their neighbors. They are skilled warriors, so we are always wary of them. But remember, we have come here to claim all these lands for Spain—that is my purpose here, and yours too. All tribes must be brought into subjugation under the crown."

Eusebio took in this information. He understood the damage that could be done in the name of the crown. His ultimate authority was God, not the King of Spain—or the Queen Regent Mariana of Austria, as it was well known that her son, King Carlos II, was ill and mentally incapable of governing. Remembering Spain's ongoing wars and financial troubles, Eusebio shook his head. He wanted to forget that endless turmoil.

Turning his attention again to the map, Eusebio traced the lines of known Baja with his index finger. Here was a new land with new possibilities—and he had a chance of making sure it was one of peace, not war.

"I have seen Sebastián Vizcaíno's maps, but he never did prove Baja is an island. It could be a peninsula," Eusebio said.

"I am most excited to travel across land that has not yet been completely measured."

Atondo nodded, then looked at the priest thoughtfully. "It would be of great help to determine that Baja is indeed not an island. And Padre, Marques de la Laguna has made a decision. He wishes to bestow upon you the title of Royal Cartographer for this expedition. You will be our official surveyor and map-maker. Of course, you must also serve as our astronomer."

Eusebio smiled broadly. "I accept these roles and all their duties!"

For the rest of the day, the two men finalized preparations of their journey. They would be traveling together for a long time. Each man realized that in spite of their differences—one a military man, the other a priest—they had to get along.

Chapter Five

BAJA

From the deck of the *San José y San Francisco Xavier*, Eusebio leaned out and stared across the water. The brilliant sun heated his face and sea wind whipped his long hair, which was now streaked with gray. The horizon seemed to pull him toward it, and he felt a childlike exhilaration.

His boyhood dream was about to come true. It wasn't China toward which he was headed, but Baja. Still, it was the adventure he'd longed for, ever since he'd met his missionary cousin, Father Martino Martini, years before.

Storms had delayed the expedition's final launch, but now it was March of 1683, and three ships under Admiral Atondo's command cut across the high, rough waves that evened out to the flat, gray-blue surface of the Gulf of California stretching far ahead.

Don Atondo had overseen the building of three ships in the

Sinaloa River, which fed into the Gulf. Before he'd left, Eusebio wrote to the duchess:

> *On October 28 of the year 1682, we sailed on this Sea of the South, and on November 3, after a safe though somewhat long voyage of seven days, we arrived at this port of Chacala. Here we are taking on supplies for a six-month voyage to the Californias.*

He was finally on his way. Patience was a skill he'd been forced to learn and relearn. He'd faced so many delays in this journey that he'd lost count.

But now his imagination soared with joy. He might explore lands never before seen by Spanish, Italian, or Dutch men. He would introduce the indigenous people to the joy and salvation of Christ. He would create new Christian worlds!

He would not crush their spirits, like some Franciscans had done. He would not attempt to enslave them or destroy the artifacts of their religions—and he hoped to prevent the one hundred Spanish soldiers whom he accompanied on this trip from hurting anyone.

He saw all humans as equal, even the natives, who seemed comparably primitive. He would teach them about God's forgiveness and eternal life. These were the messages he was born to deliver.

And yet, this moment of euphoria was tempered by a comment by Padre Goñi.

"A good day for a missionary journey, is it not?" Eusebio had jokingly greeted Goñi, who was quieter than usual before they boarded the *San José*.

"We shall see," Goñi replied, not willing to go along with Eusebio's happy outlook. At Eusebio's quizzical face, he continued, "I don't have a good feeling about this trip, Padre Kino." He scanned the low, gray clouds. "I dreamed last night that our ship splintered apart and passengers drowned. At first they cried out and tried to hold on to each other, but they went under. I could not save them, nor myself."

Sufficiently subdued at this comment, Eusebio asked, "Do you take your dreams as omens?"

"Sometimes," Padre Goñi said solemnly. "I awoke with foreboding about our journey. I hope I am wrong."

The beauty of the sparkling turquoise bay of La Paz on Baja's eastern coast took his breath away. Eusebio had never seen such white sand. When the ships dropped anchor in the bay and the passengers finally walked on solid ground, Admiral Atondo ordered them to keep quiet and stand with him on the wide deserted beach. With great ceremony, he pushed a wooden pole deep into the sand. The Spanish flag fluttered atop it in the sea breeze, and Atondo cleared his throat.

"I proclaim Spain will now regulate the collection of pearls and precious metals on this land and shores," he began loudly. He noticed a rustling at the tree line several hundred feet away. "I proclaim all peoples who live here will be treated fairly, by myself and my men."

The soldiers shouted, "Viva Monarch of the Spains!"

The bushes continued rustling. The soldiers, along with the two priests, looked back nervously. Atondo continued, "I name this place Santísima Trinidad de la California."

Eusebio tried to remain calm as four human figures tentatively emerged from the trees. They carried spears, but otherwise appeared to be curious and unthreatening. As they approached, Eusebio stepped toward them.

"Greetings," he said, bowing slightly and hoping they understood his message, if not his words. "We come in peace."

The four men were dark skinned with long black hair. They wore only pieces of leather roughly stitched together. Eusebio looked into their eyes and they stared back with apprehension.

While Eusebio invited the natives to sit with him, the soldiers set about chopping down trees to build a small lean-to, where they could sleep at least for now. In the following days and weeks, Eusebio and Goñi planted seeds in cleared areas and began building barracks and a small chapel, where the Jesuits could perform mass.

The indigenous people at first watched these efforts with interest, then joined in to help. They gathered heavy stones for the structures and filled large clay jugs with water from nearby springs and brought them to the soldiers. They also transported firewood and clay, often balancing heavy loads on top of their heads. As payment for this labor, the Spaniards gave them food, which they received with gestures of thanks.

After a few weeks, Eusebio found paper and a candle, and he wrote to the duchess:

These natives are very lively and good-natured. They are of
fine physique, happy in disposition, always ready with a smile,
and very sociable. The men wear no clothes beyond a feature
headdress; the women are clad in skins from chest to foot. Their
complexion is slightly lighter than that of the people of New
Spain, though a little boy who called upon us recently was dis-
tinctly red of skin. For food, they live mainly upon shellfish,
fruits, venison, rabbits, and birds, of which there is a great vari-
ety. The weapons employed by them are bows and arrows, with
flints unpoisoned (which they know not of). Knives and any
ironware appeal to them much, and every sort of bead, ribbon,
and decorative trifle.

Eusebio and Goñi established friendly relationships with
people of the tribes with gifts, cooked beans, and barley, and
by attempting to mimic their language. During the day, they
baptized children; in the evenings, Eusebio worked on his maps
while whole families watched over his shoulder in fascination.
Every night, the priests spent hours in prayer and took turns
reading psalms from the Bible.

One night, a shout rose up from the soldiers' camp. The
two priests ran out and found Spanish soldiers holding a Guaycura man, claiming he'd shot a Spaniard with his bow and arrow.
Atondo ordered the man to be held captive, and his men shoved
him into a cage-like structure.

"What shall we do with him?" one of Atondo's men asked.

"He should work for us," another snarled. "He can get our

water, chop our wood—why not? Isn't that what these people are good for?"

Eusebio noticed the cruelty in this comment and sensed it could lead to trouble.

That night, it was discovered that the ship boy, who'd traveled with the Spanish all the way to Baja, was missing from the camp. Atondo's men quickly speculated that he'd been kidnapped—or even killed—by one of the tribes.

Early the next morning, the Guaycura sent a group of representatives to plead for the release of the young man in the cage. Atondo's men demanded they first explain what had happened to the boy.

Confused by this question, the Guaycura men had no answer. They stood together facing the soldiers, then looked around for one of the priests to help explain what was going on.

Atondo glared at them. He had never trusted them, and now he sensed they had killed the boy. He ordered his soldiers to shoot off a nearby cannon. He merely wanted to frighten off the Guaycura men, but his soldiers misunderstood and aimed the cannon right at them.

Eusebio ran forward. "No, no! Do not harm them!" he shouted.

But it was too late. Two cannons boomed directly at the unsuspecting Guaycura men. Six fell to the ground, and three were killed instantly. The others, some only teenagers, staggered away, wounded and disoriented. Eusebio ran to the aid of the survivors, but they pushed him away and wanted nothing to do with him.

A howl made Eusebio turn to the young captive man, who frantically shook the wood frame of the cage. Eusebio ran to him amidst the chaos and sliced through the cage's thick rope door with a knife. The young man bolted, running with his people into the hills beyond the settlement.

Following the incident, a current of uneasiness flowed through Admiral Atondo's encampment. No one felt safe, including the priests. Even Atondo kept a watchful eye toward the trees and hilltops, wary of a surprise retaliatory attack. But neither the Guaycura nor the Cora tribes came near the encampment or the Jesuit chapel again.

Hunger added to the tension. Supplies were running low and the food they did have was spoiled. The ship that was supposed to arrive with fresh food was overdue, and the men assumed it had sunk.

Fearing starvation, they complained to and about Admiral Atondo, and argued among themselves. They wanted to eat and they wanted their money.

As Eusebio sat by the fire, heating water for tea, he listened to two men trade accusations over the disappearance of a small piece of meat. It had long been obvious to the priests that Atondo's men were avaricious pearl hunters more than true soldiers. When the argument escalated, Eusebio rose to intervene before serious trouble started.

"Your dream was right," he said to Padre Goñi after the bickering men had disbanded. "We are not unified; we have splintered into groups."

Padre Goñi nodded grimly.

Eusebio thought about the comet he'd seen in Cádiz. Was this the bad fortune it had signaled?

Atondo decided they must depart La Paz and return to Mexico's mainland to regroup before expanding their explorations of Baja. He wanted horses, saddles, guns, and protective armor—he needed to be prepared for hostile tribes.

Eusebio wrote to the duchess, telling her about the Cora and Guaycura tribes, assuring her they were good people with many fine qualities—openness, intelligence, and a willingness to be helpful, unless they were met with violence or deceit.

He worked on a series of maps of areas he'd traveled, and included one with his letter to the duchess, urging her to persuade her royal friends to fund Atondo's ships. He then sent letters to several Jesuit missions, asking for funding as well. The natives were friendly, he insisted, ready and willing to be converted.

In just a few months, their ships were fully loaded with food and other supplies. Eusebio and Goñi embarked with the admiral's men, heading once again to Baja, this time farther north.

They dropped anchor in another stunningly beautiful bay on October 6, the feast day for Saint Bruno. To honor the saint, Atondo named the area San Bruno, and again planted a flag for Spain.

Eusebio and Goñi placed a wooden cross in the sand and, along with Atondo and his men, knelt before it to pray for a more successful venture this time. Eusebio prayed that the soldiers had learned their violence made them all less safe. He wasn't sure they had.

At first they saw no native people, then about twenty young men and boys suddenly appeared. Curious and friendly, they sat down with the Spanish men and padres as if they'd known them for years. Eusebio showed the boys a crucifix and spoke kindly to them. They, in turn, led the padres to a spring of fresh water.

This was a good beginning. Atondo sent one of the ships back to Mexico with a message for the viceroy: they had found a hill on which a settlement could be built. It had spring water nearby and natives who appeared to be friendly.

Eusebio and Goñi walked around this place called San Bruno. Yes, the climate was blistering hot, but the people—tribes called the Didius, the Noys, and the Edues—were friendly and showed them edible fruit and nuts. They were tall and strong. The Edues cacique was called Ibo, or "the sun," and he was powerfully built with a gentle nature. When a boy from his tribe stole a small silver box from the Spanish men, Ibo ordered him to return it. For this gesture of goodwill, Atondo gave Ibo a small sharp knife, which impressed the chief.

Though they carried bows and sharp arrows, Ibo and his people showed no animosity toward the white men. But a few were wary, especially when the Spanish brought their horses ashore—never having seen the animal before, they kept a safe distance.

"They are like us in most ways," Goñi commented one night, reflecting on the natives' demeanor.

"Yes, I've seen them laugh with each other, share food,

help ones who are sick—and the families are especially close," Eusebio agreed.

"And yet they are completely different from any people I have ever encountered," Goñi said, thinking of the tribes' child-like innocence. "They eat with their hands while sitting on the ground. They wear little clothing without embarrassment. I confess, this is not easy for me—I will never get used to seeing women walk about uncovered!"

Eusebio laughed. "I understand. But think of them as our flock, and we are their protection—particularly against the sol-diers' temptations to force themselves upon them. This is a great danger."

"Yes, I thought our work was to bring Christ to the native people, but it seems it is also to remind our Spanish friends of their Christian beliefs."

Eusebio prayed Atondo's men did not antagonize the natives. Indeed, this time the admiral kept his men occupied with work, and ordered the ships to set sail for the mainland right away to ensure new supplies would be forthcoming. Peace reigned—for now.

The brown and green mountains beckoned to Eusebio. *How far away are they?* he wondered. *How far away is the Pacific Ocean?*

His desire to explore grew stronger until he finally gained permission from Admiral Atondo to set off on an exploration. He gathered supplies and a group of men to head as far west as they could. Eusebio convinced native men to travel with them as guides, and he hoped they might help if they encountered unfriendly tribes.

After weeks of slow horseback travel, the group came upon a small river, which Eusebio named Río Santo Tomás, and a marsh fed by a much-welcomed freshwater spring. Noticing a thin line of smoke rising in the distance, Eusebio and his companions aimed toward it. They were surprised to come upon a large settlement—or *ranchería*, as the Spanish called the native villages—of the Cochimí tribe. Their homes, thatched with branches, each with a hole in the center for smoke to escape from their cooking fires, filled the valley.

The Cochimí were curious, nervous, and excited at the sight of the group—and much more fearful of the horses than the men. Eusebio dismounted and pulled gifts of little wood crosses and gemstones from his bag. Padre Goñi offered food and seeds for planting, and soon the Cochimí and the explorers were mingling and exchanging words of greeting and thanks that neither could understand. Eusebio pointed west and asked the about the distance to Pacific, but he was not understood.

After this meeting, Eusebio led his group back through mountainous trails to San Bruno, where they were received warmly by Atondo and the other soldiers who had stayed behind. Each exploration gave the admiral more information of the landmarks, water sources, and friendliness of tribes—all valuable if this was to become a lasting Spanish colony.

Eusebio and Goñi settled into a routine in San Bruno, teaching the less timid natives Christian songs and the names of saints. Goñi set up small icons that depicted Mary holding the infant Jesus, which children found particularly interesting.

Eusebio tried diligently to learn the tribal languages, but without knowing a word, he gave them seeds of melon, corn, and beans. Using gestures, he explained how to grow the plants, but the soil was not good, so nothing sprouted. And because food was often scarce, Eusebio often had nothing else he could share.

The native men taught the soldiers how to hunt and fish, sharing their catches freely. Eusebio noted these gestures of goodwill and increasingly felt protective of the tribes. He was constantly on watch for a sign of violence or subjugation from the Spanish. When some tribal families were discovered sleeping near the Jesuit residence, Atondo wanted them to leave, but Eusebio prevailed in allowing them to stay. He performed baptisms, which both pleased and bewildered the native men and women.

Admiral Atondo was never as confident as Eusebio that these peoples' motives were good. He wanted little to do with them. When a young man was caught stealing food from the soldiers' camp, Atondo ordered him flogged, ignoring Eusebio's protests.

After a long, difficult summer, Atondo was awakened one morning by excited shouts. When he stepped out to see what the commotion was for, he saw that one of his ships—the *Almiranta*—had just arrived with new men, fresh supplies, and letters. Among the passengers was Padre Juan Bautista Copart, who made his way through the crowd of greeters on the beach to find Eusebio.

"Welcome, welcome!" Eusebio said, showing his Jesuit brother where he would stay. He talked about their experiences with the tribes as they walked.

Suddenly, Eusebio stopped. "Padre, I have a very specific request," he said solemnly. "I wish to make my final vows as a priest, if you will do me the honor. I know that at thirty-nine I am old—but, I trust, not too old."

"Of course," Padre Copart said. "I had assumed you had already taken your final vows! You have demonstrated beyond doubt that you are a professed Jesuit. Let us perform the ceremony tomorrow."

Admiral Atondo tended to see life with harsh realism, though Eusebio considered him unduly pessimistic; Eusebio's outlook was naturally positive, but Atondo considered him naïve. Yet the two men shared a passion: they loved exploring the mountains like two adventurous boys, and they both wanted to find a trail that led to the Pacific Ocean. On one treacherous trip in 1685, they found it.

Eager to explore the surrounding region, Eusebio and Atondo had made many short but frequent expeditions into the mountains. They had discovered crystal-clear lakes, rushing streams, and deep, dry arroyos. They found deer that were easy to shoot and kill for food. They encountered tribes who were wary and fierce; overriding Atondo's wishes, Eusebio offered them gifts and kind words to diffuse potential conflict.

It was December when the two men set out from San Bruno to blaze a trail all the way to the Pacific, taking with them more than two dozen soldiers and men from three different tribes as scouts and guides. They also brought strong horses and mules loaded with supplies.

But the going was far more difficult than they expected. The steep mountain slopes were dense with brush that had to be hacked through with machetes—a laborious task. It was nearly impossible for the horses to navigate the boulders and sharp rocks, and many of them stumbled and broke their legs, which meant they had to be shot.

After several difficult weeks, they descended the western side of the mountain range and trekked across a wide, flat stretch of hard sand. When they finally caught sight of the turquoise Pacific Ocean sparkling in the distance, they picked up their pace, at last revived.

The men tossed off their shoes, running over the sand and into the warm water, splashing and laughing like children. Black flies circled around kelp that had washed ashore. It was hot, but the ocean's cool breezes were welcome relief.

Eusebio stared out at the horizon. He'd grown a dark beard and his face was crisscrossed with scratches from sharp tree branches and insect bites. He marveled at the great expanse before him, and at the meaning of his arrival.

He and Atondo were the first Europeans to make this journey. He was tired and weary. Yet he rejoiced—he'd reached the Pacific Ocean at last. *Whether Baja is an island or a peninsula,* he thought, *we have just crossed its width, from one sea to another.*

Three men tried, to no avail, to dislodge a giant whale bone from the sand to bring back with them. Meanwhile, the tribesmen gathered large blue shells scattered over the sand. Eusebio picked one up to examine it closely, and admired its shiny color. "Why do you collect these?" he asked.

"We use them for drinking," replied one man, as if it were obvious.

Eusebio climbed a sand dune to soak in the vast scene. Billowy white clouds sitting above the sea gave way to a stark blue sky. Waves lapping gently onto the sand calmed his mind.

A rustle behind Eusebio made him turn around just in time to see about fifteen young native men duck and run toward the trees. They were from a tribe he did not recognize. He stood to call out to them with the few words he'd learned at the San Bruno settlement, but they would not show themselves.

Eusebio reached into his bag and pulled out some handkerchiefs and some necklaces made of colored glass. He'd brought them just for this purpose. To his left, fifteen more young men peeked out from another stand of trees.

"We come in peace!" Eusebio shouted with a smile. Hearing this, Atondo climbed the dune and he too called out to the tribesmen.

"We have gifts!" Atondo said. With Eusebio, he walked slowly toward the timid people, who ran farther away.

"Let us leave the gifts here," Eusebio said. He draped the necklaces and other items on the twisted bushes that dotted the dunes. Atondo placed a pair of shoes on the ground, along with a wooden box containing beads. Then they stepped away, back toward the sea.

From a distance, they watched as twenty or thirty men

appeared, all barely clothed with smooth skin darkened by the sun, and rushed to examine the gifts. After glancing warily at Atondo and Eusebio, the natives took the items, then hurried back to the trees, disappearing for good.

That night, after tossing and turning, Eusebio got up and took a walk in the moonlight. He was used to the silence, even comfortable in it. He could feel God's presence wrapped around him like the cool breezes that brushed against his shoulders and face. He was attuned to the little noises here—a far-off owl's hoot, the rustle of a fox on the hunt.

He climbed a small hill and sat down to look over the valley. It was then that he heard a sound like a distant bubbling stream—he recognized it as human voices whispering. From where he sat, he could see a desert valley punctuated with ocotillo and saguaro cacti. To his right, the vast Pacific glistened in the moonlight. His black cassock was torn in places, and covered with sand, which had also found its way into his hair, eyes, and the lines on his face.

The lush hills of northern Italy were thousands of miles away, and the contrast between this desert and his village home of Segno made him smile. The rhythms here fascinated him: blazing hot days followed by glowing sunsets and surprisingly chilly nights. He'd seen huge lightning bolts flashing through clouds at night, waves of black flies sweeping over the beach, scorpions darting out of his path in the sand, wide vistas of water and sand, and no sign of human life. Parched by the sun's heat, he feared running out of drinking water . . . yet he was strangely drawn to this place.

There it was again—a young woman's voice, or maybe a child whispering. Without turning his head, Eusebio discerned native people behind him somewhere, watching. Spanish soldiers viewed these indigenous people as enemies or as potential slave labor. Eusebio assumed nothing and tried to see every person as Jesus did.

He turned his gaze to the sky and located the constellations, as vivid and close as if they glowed on a cabin ceiling. Again, he smiled. Never in his years in Italy, Germany, or Spain had he imagined that stars and planets could appear this close or so bright.

Now he could distinguish the whispering voices were male and female. And they were getting closer. Slowly, Eusebio looked over his shoulder. There stood three young people in their early twenties, two men and a woman, who were short in stature. They had long, thick hair and wore simple cotton pieces loosely stitched together. Were they siblings? They gripped small spears, but their expressions were open, even childlike. Eusebio smiled and waved. He did not move as the three carefully stepped toward him as if he were a tiger that might pounce any moment.

"Hello," Eusebio said, nodding. "*Buenas noches.*" One of the young men replied in his native language.

Spanish soldiers had tricked native men into diving for pearls, then stealing all they found—it was wise of the natives to keep themselves at a safe distance. Yet Eusebio had been sent with explicit instructions to improve the lives of the desert people in matters temporal and spiritual. He was to help them build sturdier houses, grow food more efficiently, and save precious water—as well as introduce the simple concepts of Christianity and baptize them in the name of Christ. Baja sorely needed this.

Now he studied his young visitors' faces as they drew closer. "I am admiring God's work in the heavens above," he said cheerfully, knowing they could not understand him. "God, who made these stars and planets, made us too—you and me."

He gestured broadly to the dark sky, then to himself and to them. They watched him curiously. He reached into his pocket and pulled out a maple wooden cross. It was just a few inches long and smooth to the touch. He held it up, then reached out, indicating that he wanted to give it to them.

The older of the two men stepped forward and gently took the cross. He spoke for a few minutes in his language, then stepped back. The three turned the cross over in their hands. Then, timidly, the young woman took something from a pouch slung over her shoulder and reached toward Eusebio.

Understanding immediately the significance of the gift, Eusebio accepted the object—a large blue abalone shell, just like the ones he'd seen earlier that day, that glowed in the moonlight. Obviously, these shells were associated with this part of the shoreline.

"Thank you," he said, looking in her eyes. "I will keep this forever and treasure it."

Suddenly, a loud whoop rose up in the distance, and a gunshot fired into the night. The three natives dropped to a low crouch and Eusebio scanned the darkened landscape. Far off, where Atondo's soldiers had set up a base camp from which to explore the surrounding mountains, Eusebio saw figures lurch in front of a campfire. What were they doing? The shouting was followed by guffaws, then another gunshot.

When Eusebio turned back, the three had vanished. He looked around, then down at the shell. He closed his fingers over it and began to find his way back down through the rocks to the desert camp.

He prayed in the name of missionary Saint Francis Xavier, who had endured much more than this before he died on a Chinese island more than a century before. *May it please the supreme and divine goodness to give me abundant grace, ever to know his most holy will, and perfectly to fulfill it.*

He imagined Saint Francis Xavier walking beside him. Eusebio had always felt a deep kinship with the saint. Francis Xavier had been a free-living young man in Paris when he met Ignatius of Loyola, who transformed his life. The two established the Society of Jesus and Xavier became an intrepid missionary, enduring tremendous hardship and disappointment in Asia, where he died. Eusebio felt the saint could be his brother, they were so alike.

How can I possibly succeed with so much against me? Eusebio wondered, thinking of the violent Spanish soldiers and the wariness of the natives.

With God's help, came the answer. Eusebio heard it in his heart, not his ears. In the distance, a chorus of coyotes began a frenzied yipping.

~

The return journey to San Bruno was arduous for Atondo, Eusebio, and their men. But now that they'd attained their goal of reaching the other side of Baja, their mood was light, even joyous. They reached San Bruno tired and hungry, but in good spirits. But they were met with solemn news: the ship with supplies still had not arrived, probably delayed by storms. Once again, food was dangerously scarce.

It had been many months since Atondo's men had been paid, and though the shore waters were rich with fish, they had found no pearls—one reason Marques de la Laguna had been willing to underwrite this venture.

An important decision had to be made, and though disappointment weighed heavily upon his mind, Atondo knew what it would be. He abhorred the idea of defeat, but they would have to abandon San Bruno.

"Why now?" asked Eusebio, who'd visited the admiral's lean-to a week after their triumphant return from the Pacific. "After all we've suffered and achieved, why leave? Surely the supplies will arrive soon."

"I cannot risk the death of my men—some are becoming ill," Atondo replied, his dark brows furrowed. He'd wanted Eusebio to know his decision before anyone else, but he found the priest's argument tiresome. "The men are angry and hungry. There is no silver in these hills, and no pearls in the waters. We have explored areas north and south, but there is no place suitable for a sustainable colony. Life is hard here; I see no sign of it getting better." Lowering his voice, he said, "I've received word that the viceroy has withdrawn further financial support. He needs his money to subdue the tribes just north of Mexico City."

"Subdue them?" Eusebio said. His reaction was so angry that Atondo looked up in surprise. "What have Padre Goñi and I done but subdue these people? Not with not force, but with kindness and the simplest gifts—food, a piece of glass, a cotton scarf. And as the Bible suggests," Eusebio went on, looking directly into the admiral's eyes, "catching men to become followers of Christ is more fruitful than catching pearls. The natives here are ready and willing to be converted! If we leave now, our efforts will be for nothing."

"Not for nothing," Atondo replied, too uncomfortable to look at Eusebio. "You have proved your approach works, though you have converted fewer people than I had hoped. But I will sing your praises to the viceroy, and it will help you in your work in Mexico."

"So, we really are abandoning this settlement." Eusebio, exasperated, ran his hands through his long hair.

"Yes, Padre. For now," Atondo said.

Within a month, the Spanish colonists pulled apart the structures they had so faithfully built, packed their belongings, and helped the sickest among them get onto the ships. Finally, they boarded the horses and mules.

It was a cool morning in May 1686 when Eusebio solemnly bade goodbye to his native friends. Two young men who had been baptized by the priests cried. Eusebio's emotions welled up in his chest, but he held back tears. *This is not the ending any missionary wants*, he thought.

As he headed to the beach where rowboats waited, the priest's eye caught sight of Atondo leaving his men to slip back toward the now-empty dwellings. A young native woman carrying a baby stepped toward him. Eusebio watched in amazement as Atondo spoke to the woman, then leaned down and kissed the baby, whose skin was a lighter shade of brown than its mother. Then Atondo caressed the young woman's upturned face and hurried back to the waiting rowboat.

Eusebio shook his head and followed the admiral, climbing into the rowboat that would take them to the waiting ship. Twenty people watched in silence from the shore as the Spanish men and two priests left the bay to return to Mexico.

Padre Goñi and Eusebio leaned over the rail of the ship's deck, staring out at the white-capped waves. Sails full, the ship cut briskly across the water.

"I am disappointed, of course," Goñi said. "These lands need the presence of missionaries like us. I pray for God to show me the right place, but I have come to love Mexico City and I hope to stay there."

"Our work in Baja was just beginning—we could have done more," Eusebio said. "My hope is to discover new lands and live peaceably with these tribes—and protect them from the Spanish. These tribes are much wiser than most think. They have a natural spiritual inclination that we can guide toward Christianity."

The two men fell silent and looked out across the Gulf of California. The ship headed south, toward Acapulco. They were no longer idealistic missionaries. They had suffered a defeat, and they had to find a way to do the impossible.

Chapter Six

DEMANDING JUSTICE

Eusebio arrived in the coastal town of Acapulco, the land's second most-important port after Vera Cruz. This was the city where ships carrying exotic goods from Asia stopped—making the surrounding waters attractive to pirates.

Acapulco was a pleasant town, but Eusebio was eager to begin the 185-mile journey north to Mexico City. He stopped at Jesuit missions along the way, across the Yaqui territory.

It was a bittersweet return to the familiar Jesuit residence in Mexico City, the very place from which Eusebio had launched into his long-awaited missionary work just two years before. The Baja natives were uppermost in his mind and he prayed constantly that they would not be abandoned forever. Prayer never failed to calm and focus his mind.

When Atondo found Eusebio after some time visiting with officials, he explained there was no going back to Baja. Atondo had been told in no uncertain terms that all funds were being reallocated to paying off Spain's debt to France.

Now what? Eusebio could not stay in this city; it was already stifling his restless spirit. He sat in the silence of the cool, dark chapel. It was comforting to be back in this solid stone place with its small altar. He knelt before it and waited, eyes closed, hoping the Holy Ghost would reveal his next step. His own heartbeat filled the quiet.

China, his longtime dream, had slipped from his missionary goals. For months, he had harbored a secret wish that he'd receive a message from Spain to board a ship for Asia. But now he didn't even think about going there anymore. The dry, rocky landscapes and natives with their simple yet good life here in New Spain intrigued him and captured his imagination.

Certainly, the hardships were great—but Francis Xavier and Ignatius had established that suffering was part of missionary work. Living and working among the sick and poor, despite the risks of hunger and thirst—this was what he wanted. Eusebio accepted the necessary burdens.

What he did not like was the petty jockeying for power among some of the Jesuit bishops. Inwardly, he struggled with the rule of obedience when it came to dealing with such men. Here in New Spain, they wanted control over the expanding territories and they angled for power—Eusebio loathed this foolish maneuvering. It was a waste of time. He'd seen how the many tribes were willing to be converted, given the right circumstances—this was their purpose.

Eusebio crossed himself and rose to his feet. Without

question, he knew his next step. He would apply to Padre Luis del Canto, the provincial of the Jesuits in New Spain, to go into the Sonoran Desert—a harsh, forbidding region in northwestern Mexico—to live and work among the tribes.

Within days, Marques de la Laguna received Padre Canto's request on behalf of Padre Eusebio Kino. An old man with a salt-and-pepper beard, the viceroy read the letter that asked for his approval. He nodded as he read. He had long wanted the Sonoran to be colonized—perhaps this Jesuit would pave the way by subduing the savages.

He wrote back to Padre Canto saying he wholeheartedly supported Padre Kino's wish.

"How I wish you were here to discuss my adventures," Eusebio wrote. It was March 1687, and he was resting in a room at the Jesuit residence in the small village of Opusura, scratching out a letter to the duchess with black ink on a piece of parchment.

He had finally left the City of Mexico to head north toward the Sonoran Desert. It was a long, arduous journey with his small group of newly arrived Jesuit priests and a few servants. He'd been given permission to devote his full attention to the people who lived in regions where few Spanish dared to settle.

He smiled as he described to the duchess the cool freshwater at Lake Chapala and the town of Guadalajara, where an elegant cathedral was nearly half built. He wrote about how on the first night at a campfire, a young priest told him that the owners of silver mines had trapped men of the tribes to do the most dangerous and backbreaking work. The man had described their cruelty in detail, claiming this violence naturally instilled terror in the native men and made it impossible to approach them for Christian teaching. A coil of anger tightened in Eusebio's chest at this story.

Upon reaching Guadalajara the next day, he made his way to a low adobe structure that served as a government office. An old man who served as secretary was dozing when Eusebio entered, and he woke up in a confused state when he saw a priest standing before him.

"I have come to make a formal request for royal provisions to establish missionary settlements in the region," Eusebio told him. "And I need to see the highest official here to lodge a complaint."

"Oh, yes, go to the room at the end of hall," the man said. "Captain Zeballos will see you."

"Zeballos?" Eusebio had not heard the name before.

"He is the king's representative," the old man said, now fully awake and suddenly officious. He glared at Eusebio as if to fend off an argument.

Eusebio strode confidently into the office of Captain Zeballos and introduced himself, then he got right to the point. "You probably know native people are being enslaved in the silver mines, held against their will, and forced to work without pay. This is not Christian," he said accusingly. "It is wrong and it must stop. If they choose to work in the mines, they must be paid a wage, like any Spanish man."

Zeballos raised an eyebrow at this outburst from a priest with wild hair and dusty clothes. "Do you not know King Carlos has issued a royal decree about this?" he asked, as if indulging a child.

"No . . . I do not," Eusebio said, surprised.

"The decree grants any native who chooses conversion immunity from slave labor for twenty years," Zeballos said. "You may use it, if it helps. But be careful, Padre. It will not make the Spanish mine owners happy."

Eusebio wrote all this to the duchess; he was now on his second piece of paper:

Several days later, we came upon the silver mining camp of San Juan Bautista. We arrived just in time to witness the Spanish owner—a short but strong man—jabbing the natives with a sharp stick as they worked. When one tried to escape, he was dragged back over the rocks by his hair and brutally kicked and whipped.

He stopped writing. Would this vivid description upset the duchess? Then he remembered how she looked directly into his eyes and always wanted to hear the truth, so he continued writing:

I jumped from my horse to intervene, but the mine owner touched his gun and suggested I mind my own business and keep moving.

When I saw the gun, I kept my distance but loudly announced that I'd come with a decree from the His Majesty. I pulled the paper out of my saddlebag and held it up to see. I told him, through my interpreter, that my priests and I would offer these natives the chance for a Christian education. Those who wished to be converted would be set free forever. Those who declined would continue working in his mine. A bit of confusion and chaos ensued, but ultimately all the natives were released into the care of a Jesuit priest who has a small school nearby. They can return to their families—and never work in a mine again—as long as they study with him for two hours each day.

As I left the mine, two women approached me. They were the wife and daughter of the mine owner, and they whispered thanks for what I had done. They were greatly disturbed by the treatment of the natives but were powerless to change the mine owner's behavior. I saw in these women the same goodness I find in you.

He lifted his pen from the paper and gazed out his small window. It seemed that God had used him to save these people. Eusebio remembered how the duchess smiled when he told her of his missionary dreams of saving souls, as if she were living her own dreams through his. Now they were finally coming true. Yet it was also clear that he had to stop the violence if he were to establish real trust of the tribes.

I think of you often. I pray you are healthy, that your life in Cádiz is pleasant. Please, pray for me that my work bears fruit

here. I continue to write as often as I can with faith that at least
some of my letters will reach you.
Your friend and servant,
Eusebio Kino

Chapter Seven

PIMA

It was hot, and the dusty trails were covered with sharp brown rocks. Plodding mules, weighed down with water jugs and supplies, stumbled along between the saguaro cacti and agave.

Lulled by the heat and the necessarily slow pace, the travelers lapsed into silence. Shielded from the blazing sun by a wide-brimmed hat, Eusebio fell into dark thoughts. *Is death waiting for me out in the Sonoran Desert? Is a poisoned arrow aimed at my heart somewhere out there?*

His eye caught a movement: a rattlesnake slithered out of the way of his horse.

Eusebio had received a letter from Padre Manuel González, the father superior of the western district of Mexico. He was ordered to go into the Pimería Alta—an area encompassing the Sonoran and uncharted deserts to the northwest. The area was inhabited by Pima, Papago, Sobaípuri, and Yuma tribes. Eusebio's curiosity and fear grew. Who were these people?

Though an old man, Padre González offered to accompany Eusebio, who enthusiastically welcomed his superior's companionship. Another Jesuit, Padre José de Aguilar, a missionary of the Ópatas in Cucurpe, offered to join too. The three met at an outdoor table in the village of Oposura before their departure date.

"I want to find a location deep within the Pimería Alta for my residence and mission," Eusebio said as they ate a breakfast of cornbread and fruit. "But I have heard some tribes are hostile to outsiders. They already have stories about kidnapping by the Spanish. Their borders are known only to them—we can't see when we enter into their territories, so this journey will be dangerous."

Padre Aguilar, a slim Spaniard with dark, lively eyes, had been educated in Spain before arriving in Mexico. "They fear priests—all priests, not just Jesuits—believing we seek the death of their medicine men or spiritual leaders," he said.

"They are right!" Padre González said, shaking his head. "Some priests have used violence and force in the name of Christianity, destroying any chance of true conversion of the Pima or the people of any other tribe, who otherwise would have benefitted from our guidance."

"There is another danger," Aguilar said. "I'm sure you know, the Apaches and their allies are constantly fighting Spanish ranchers. Apache tribes have stolen horses, which now give them speed of travel. And they have stolen cattle, which they now raise themselves for food. It's difficult to say which side is more ruthless, the Apaches or the Spanish soldiers—each murder and plunder on a large scale."

"We have to make our intentions clear—that we wish to help, to teach the way of Christ," Eusebio said, but his usual optimism was dampened by hearing this news of violence in the Sonora region. The men fell silent, their minds heavy with the danger and difficulty of the task.

After their breakfast in Oposura, they organized the men they had hired for the trip—men who could help interpret the Pima language and help load horses and mules for the new adventure into the Valley of Sonora.

Spring in the desert brought wildflowers that bloomed among the rocks. Even the cacti sprouted cheerful yellow and pink flowers. In the distance, gray-green hills gave way to the sharp silhouette of mountains. A black vulture soared overhead in the afternoon sky. Puffy white clouds hung low near the horizon.

By late afternoon on a day in March 1687, Eusebio, González, and Aguilar safely entered Cucurpe, a little village near a stand of large sycamore trees. They had now crossed into Upper Pima—the Pimería Alta. The Jesuits and their assistants prepared sleeping mats beneath a sycamore tree, then made a campfire meal of beans and cooked rabbit.

"Tell me, Padre Aguilar," Eusebio said as he positioned his saddle as a pillow. "Tell me the names of all the tribes who live here."

"Pima, Sobaípuri, Papago, and Soba people all speak the same language," Aguilar replied. "To the north are Yuma tribes, the Coco Maricopa, Quíquima, Cócopa. I have heard of tribes called Tepoca and Seri, but I don't know much about them."

Eusebio contemplated these names and marveled at the people who had built an extended network of villages here. *Perhaps for centuries*, he speculated. Yet he was certain no professor of history in his beloved Ingolstadt university had ever heard of these tribes.

Eventually, the campfire sputtered and stars became visible in the darkening sky, twinkling between the tree branches overhead. But sleep did not come easily. Eusebio lay on his mat, staring at the night sky while his companions snored. He looked for the constellations—they always reminded him of his cousin Martino.

A shooting star streaked silently across the vast darkness. Eusebio smiled, remembering his long-standing argument with Don Carlos de Sigüenza y Góngora about the comet. And he remembered Sor Juana Inés de la Cruz, the nun who wrote poems and who had a dim view of men. How unusual she was. Those first years in Mexico City seemed long ago and far away.

May this shooting star be a sign that this journey into the desert with the Pima is blessed by God, Eusebio thought. No other Christian had ventured this far into these desert lands, which held as much danger and risk as potential reward.

Eusebio's eyelids drifted closed, and he felt a deep fatigue throughout his body. Though covered with a warm wool blanket, he had the sensation of standing at the edge of the world. One more step and he would float among the stars that seemed to draw him up and out. His heart filling with a childlike happiness, he fell asleep.

At dawn the next morning, the three Jesuits held mass and shared a meager breakfast at their campfire. Then they set out again, heading north along the sparkling San Miguel River, which rushed with spring mountain water. The men found their way up a long, sloping promontory that overlooked the valley ahead.

They were unprepared for the sweeping view from the top: a vast *ranchería* of Pima people in two fertile valleys that bordered fields of corn, squash, beans, melons, and even watermelons. As Eusebio surveyed the scene, one of his men said the Pima called this place Cósari.

"Cósari," he repeated, taking a deep breath. The land was filled with beauty and promise. He remembered the shooting star the night before. "Here is where we will build our first mission," he said to Aguilar and González. "I want to call it Nuestra Señora de los Dolores, or Our Lady of Sorrows, for the native tribes have suffered greatly at the hands of the Spanish."

"My friend, this is an auspicious time for a new beginning," Padre González said. "I am confident you have found the right location for your first mission here in the Pimería Alta. I will take my leave and return to Guadalajara. Please send word about your progress."

Eusebio bowed his head in deference to Padre González. "*Vaya con dios!*" he called out as the old man and his servant guided their horses and mule back out into the hot desert from which they'd come.

Facing Padre Aguilar, Eusebio said, "Let us now find the cacique and ask his permission to establish our mission here."

A great commotion erupted when the Pima saw them coming. Though some men picked up bows and arrows, others gaped at the sight of the strange men: Black Robes. No one knew how fast and far information traveled among the tribes, but stories about the Jesuits had been told and retold.

The crowd parted and their cacique boldly stepped forward. He was a striking figure, a muscular man of about forty with sharp dark eyes and long black hair. His name was Coxi. He greeted the Jesuit group without a smile, yet he did not appear threatened.

Eusebio and Aguilar immediately dismounted their horses to share gifts from their bags—glass beads, seeds, and wooden crosses. Coxi received the gifts tentatively, turning them over in his hands, then passing them around to the men, women, children, and elders who stood with him. Though poor, the Pima appeared well fed and peaceful. The Jesuits scanned the scene— whole generations, from babies to grandparents, apparently lived together in one large community.

Spreading out his arms, a gesture he'd learned long ago from his Italian parents, Eusebio did his best to communicate friendliness. He explained that they wished to sleep in a grove of trees just outside the settlement. Coxi nodded and spoke in a way that sounded like words of welcome.

As they unpacked their horses and mules, the crowd watched them in fascination. Seeing he had an audience, Eusebio talked to them about God and Jesus, the great peacemaker. He pointed to the sky, to his own chest, and to the Pima before him and said, "We are all children of God. May blessings be upon you."

"Padre, not one of them understands a word you are saying," Aguilar said with a smile.

"I know," Eusebio replied cheerfully, "but I think they understand my meaning just the same. I want them to know we are peaceful—I do not want to wait until I am proficient in their language to try conveying that message."

The Pima watched, and at times giggled, as the Jesuits began setting up a temporary camp in the shade of the trees.

In the following days, Aguilar and Eusebio traveled to three more Pima *rancherías*—one called Caborica, where they promised to establish a mission named after Saint Ignatius of Loyola, and another inhabited by Ymuris where they planned the mission of Saint Joseph. The third they agreed to call Nuestra Señoras de los Remedios. Then they returned to Mission Dolores.

Three small brown faces, barely containing their laughter, stared at Eusebio up close. As he opened his eyes, a little boy and girl burst into giggles, hopping happily around him. Eusebio and his companions had slept on the ground under the trees. Now, as they sat up, they noticed a crowd of Pima people curiously watching their every move. It was obvious that many of them had slept on the ground close by the Jesuits the night before. A teenage boy with a bright smile stepped forward and offered the priests a large clay jug filled with water. The men drank from it gratefully, then washed their faces.

"What is your name?" Eusebio asked the boy. Through much effort at interpretation, he learned it was Se-eh-ha. "Thank you for the water, Se-eh-ha."

Eusebio pulled a cross from his bag, then a small painted icon of the face of Jesus, and placed the items against a tree trunk. He and Aguilar knelt before them and began to say mass.

A whisper of excitement flew through the small crowd of onlookers. When they finished, the two padres rose and took food from their packs for breakfast. Several young boys ran off and returned with a watermelon, which they broke open with a rock. Handing the pieces to the Jesuits, they watched in delight as Eusebio and his friends ate hungrily.

"Today, we will determine the exact location for the chapel," Eusebio said to Aguilar, "then find men who can help build it."

"Padre, these people look up to us as if we are kings! We could ask them to do whatever we want."

Eusebio shook his head. "We must be careful about ordering them to do anything. We need to get to know them, sit with them, eat with them, learn their traditions. And if they do any task for us, we pay them. True conversion requires patience, tolerance, and kindness—to create a bond of trust, just as God has done with us. We could baptize everyone living in this settlement. What a treasure we have in this place!"

Aguilar smiled in admiration. He'd never known a priest to be so compassionate and determined at the same time.

A sudden commotion made the two turn around. A group of three Spanish ladies dressed in formal black dresses had just arrived in a rickety horse-drawn cart.

"Padre! Padre!" One woman nearly fell out of the cart as she called to Eusebio and Aguilar. She explained they were wives of ranch owners nearby.

"What a surprise and an honor. What brings you here, señora?" Eusebio asked.

"Padre, Holy Week begins in two days. Now that you are here, we must prepare for the procession of the Blessed Sacrament!" the oldest of the women said urgently. "The children here, well—even if you haven't baptized all of them yet, we must get them ready. We have costumes and necklaces for them, and I am sure you have some too."

"Of course," Eusebio said, looking at her with astonishment. He wanted to laugh, but he recognized these Christian women were dead serious.

Two days later, he stood amazed as the procession of more than one hundred Pima—including forty newly baptized children adorned in colorful clothes, as well as Spaniards on horseback and on foot—marched from Mission Dolores to a small nearby village.

"Oh, ye of little faith," Eusebio muttered to himself with a smile. It was a splendid and happy parade.

At the makeshift chapel, Eusebio led a proper Easter ceremony, which pleased the señoras and the priests and fascinated the curious Pima.

~

To pray alone, in a place where he was sure to be uninterrupted, Eusebio sometimes hiked into the surrounding hills. One evening, when he realized he had just a few more hours of daylight left, he hurriedly climbed a hill for this purpose. Stopping to determine the best direction, he heard a soft beating sound. He instinctively walked toward it.

Low singing accompanied the sound, and Eusebio crouched down as he approached a small clearing where a group of men sat in a circle. His heart leapt when he recognized the cacique named Coxi. The chief sat on a rock in the midst of fourteen other men seated around him, several of whom beat a complex rhythm on small drums. Eusebio parted the branches of a tree to get a clear view.

The drum-beating stopped and Coxi stood, holding up a long black feather. He turned several times with the feather, singing a low, almost moaning, song. The men in the circle repeated the song; they and Coxi went back and forth like this for a while. Then the chief reached down and began to speak, gesturing dramatically to the sky, the trees, and the ground. Eusebio sensed he was telling a story. Coxi picked up a tiny clay jar of a red substance and smeared some of it onto his right hand. He approached each man in the circle and touched their foreheads, smearing a red mark on each of them. He held the black feather up again, turned three times, returned to the rock, and sat down.

After a brief silence, the drum-beating softly resumed. Coxi spoke for a few moments, and although Eusebio could not understand, he felt he was witnessing an important ritual. Each man in the circle looked at Coxi with fear and respect. Eusebio let the branches go and took small, silent steps backward.

He didn't need to pray for now. He saw God alive and well among these people. They had no chapels, no hierarchy of priests and bishops, no cathedrals, and no pope. Yet Chief Coxi had as deep a reverence for holy ritual as any priest in Rome.

After securing Coxi's approval, Padres Aguilar and Kino, with help from their companions, constructed a chapel using wood from the tall cottonwood trees. As the Pima demonstrated their skills in adobe building, Eusbio watched, fascinated, trying to remember each ingredient and each step in creating these cool, sturdy structures. In gratitude, he paid them with food and gifts. He already planned to build a water mill near one of the wide streams and a small house to serve as sleeping quarters—but he would need their help for these big projects. He sent a messenger to Coxi, inviting him to meet at Mission Dolores.

Coxi came by foot with two of his sons. His chest was bare, and only his lower half was covered with rough skins. He wore a thin beaded band around his strong forehead. By now, Eusebio had met with him several times and he appreciated the chief's calm, even nature. Eusebio called a servant to act as interpreter and they all sat in a circle in front of the mission.

"I honor you, Coxi, cacique of this Pima region," Eusebio began. Showing respect was critical, he knew, with all people. Chief Coxi nodded his head. His face was wrinkled and his eyes were clear and dark. "Your men have helped me with building, and I will need them to build a water mill too. May I have your permission to ask them to help me? I can offer them, and their families, food for the work."

After the interpreter told Coxi what Eusebio had asked, the chief held up his hand and said something. "He wants to know why you were watching him from behind a tree yesterday," the interpreter said.

Eusebio flushed. "I came upon the chief by accident. I meant no harm; I was curious."

Coxi spoke and the boy interpreted once again. "We hear that Black Robes want to steal our spirits and kill our medicine man. Is this true?"

"No," Eusebio said emphatically. "I am a man of peace. I don't want to steal anything from you. I want only peace. No stealing, no shooting, no killing, no harm."

The chief was silent, searching Eusebio's face for any trace of deceit. Eusebio grew uncomfortable under Coxi's intense scrutiny—he seemed to be looking for something in his soul.

Eusebio tried another tack. He pulled out three packs of wheat seeds that he'd brought from Europe and handed them to Coxi and his sons. "I will show you how to grow this abundant food," he said.

Coxi broke his gaze to examine the seeds. The Pima were skilled farmers, obvious by their well-organized fields, but they did not seem to make use of the ditch irrigation the priests had seen farther south.

"I will help you make your fields even more productive with ditches near the rivers and streams," Eusebio said. "But we need the water mill and we need your help. I will pay with food and many more seeds."

"We will help you," Coxi said. He rose and said goodbye, then he and his sons returned home.

With great care, Eusebio built trust between him and the Pima people. When he made a promise to them, he kept it. When Pima men and women worked for him, he paid them. When Pima men built adobe structures, he worked side by side with them. When the crops at Mission Dolores were harvested, the Pima received the largest portion for their families.

With the little money he had, Eusebio sent a servant to Cucurpe to purchase tools from the Spaniards; when they arrived, he taught a small group of men how to use them. He was heartened to see how quickly they learned. *I will teach them every skill I know—farming and carpentry, especially*, he thought. *What I can't teach them, I will find a man who can.*

With Mission Dolores now established, Padre Aguilar decided to visit his mission in Cucurpe. As Aguilar left, Eusebio remembered the name of a Spanish blacksmith in Guadalajara and asked Aguilar to send for him so he might teach his skills to the Pima.

"I know the man—I am happy to ask him," Aguilar said. "And I will pray for your safety and success here." He tipped his hat and rode south, turning to wave one more time to Eusebio before reaching the summit of a red rock promontory. Then he was gone.

A month later, on a hot, dry afternoon, as swirls of sand

swept through Mission Dolores, the blacksmith arrived. Instead of being happy to reach his destination, he seemed nervous and agitated, and asked to speak to Eusebio as soon as possible.

"Greetings, señor," Eusebio said, coming out of the chapel. He shook the man's hand. The blacksmith had broad shoulders and a strong grip. He clutched his dusty hat, his eyes full of worry.

"Padre, I send good wishes from the padres of Guadalajara. But on my trip, I heard people say bad things about you. It's the ranch owners and silver mine owners—they don't like what you are doing. They say you are making it hard for them to keep slaves, which they need to maintain their ranches and mines."

The blacksmith looked down. He was uncomfortable bringing bad news to a man of God.

"What are the names of these men?" Eusebio asked. A swarm of small flies came out of nowhere; he swatted them away. "I understand they wish to protect their livelihood, but I cannot support enslavement. It is not Christian, and—as they know—slavery is prohibited by the king. Any man who labors for the Spanish must do it willingly and receive pay. Any woman who works as a servant must do it willingly, with the permission of her husband, and must be paid. I will talk to them."

The blacksmith told him the names and, after bowing slightly, left to unload the tools he'd brought in saddlebags via mule. Pima men quickly gathered around him, eager to inspect the strange objects.

Eusebio squinted at the horizon, as if he expected to see the Spanish mine owners already riding their horses toward him. He knew well what angry Spanish landowners could do if they felt threatened. He'd seen their anger, their violence, and their cruel treatment of docile people. Would they feel so threated that they would do him harm?

Once the bell tower was completed, Eusebio sent for a church bell from Mexico City. It arrived six months later, to the great excitement of the Jesuits and the Pima people at the Mission Dolores. Eusebio and the blacksmith carefully hung the bell in the mission's short bell tower.

The following Sunday, the priests gathered a crowd at the mission and invited a young Pima girl to pull the bell's rope. A loud peal echoed across the valley as the Pima people shouted with delight at this exhilarating new sound.

Then a sudden crack of gunfire broke through the shouts of joy.

Eusebio instinctively hunched down and whipped his head in the direction of the shot. The crowd of Pima people drew back, terrified. Three Spanish soldiers on horseback stood about twenty yards away, smiling.

Eusebio rushed toward them. "What are you doing?" he demanded, his face set in anger.

"Don't let them get too happy, Padre," a soldier said, chewing a long stalk of grass. "You will lose control, and then—trouble."

"Get away from here before you create enemies out of friends," Eusebio said. "We are celebrating this mission—this *Christian* mission."

The soldiers smirked and stood their ground. Eusebio did not budge either, but gently pulled a wooden cross from his pocket. The soldiers watched him uneasily, then turned and left.

"I look forward to your confessions!" Eusebio shouted after them.

Months passed, and the priests prayed for the strength to complete the buildings they needed at this mission. After the chapel and bell tower were done, the small, low residence from which Eusebio would work was finished too. Its adobe walls were so thick that, even on the hottest days, the interiors were dark and cool.

Every evening, in his prayers, Eusebio envisioned the fruits of these long, hard days: missions filling the valleys and peace between all people. That was his wish, hope, and constant prayer.

He continued writing to Duchess de Aveiro, though he now received few replies. "Many of these poor people, despite their humble condition, on seeing and experiencing kind treatment, will come to rely on the missionary with deep attachment, sharing the best of their possessions and food," Eusebio wrote one evening by candlelight. He told the duchess proudly that he had learned some words of the Pima language.

But he did not write of the trouble that was brewing. Padre González had sent him a message of alarm: he'd heard rumors that natives were moving away from Mission Dolores. Eusebio wrote back immediately that this was not true; in fact, families arrived each day, wishing to live close to the Jesuits. Eusebio often awoke to find whole families had slept outside the mission.

But when he visited missions he'd established with Padre Aguilar, he found that the Pima who had once been so open and friendly were now more wary and uncommunicative. Eusebio confronted them, asking what was wrong.

Jesuit priests kill people with their holy oils for baptism, they told him. And Black Robes had lynched Pima men and were enslaving their people, forcing them to work in their fields.

"Who told you these things?" Eusebio asked.

"Two Spanish men who came on horseback to warn us," one elder replied. "They came from a ranch—from that way," he said, waving to the south. Eusebio asked the names of the Spanish men—he was not surprised they were the very names the blacksmith had given him.

"Believe what you see me do, not what other men tell you," Eusebio said solemnly. "I honor you and wish only good for you and your families. I will never hurt you."

The elder took in these words as they were interpreted to him. He focused his eyes on Eusebio and nodded his head.

Eusebio was giving thanks for Padre Aguilar's safe return when his prayers were interrupted by a woman's sharp cry. He dashed outside at the sound. The crying woman's family supported her to keep her from falling down. The native interpreter explained to Eusebio that the woman's son had been hunting with some friends in the last hours of daylight when he encountered a group of Spanish men on horses. They were drunk and tried to grab the bow and arrow from the young man's hands, but he would not let go. Without warning, one of the Spanish men pulled out his gun and shot the young Pima. They laughed as they left. The boy's friends had rushed to his side, but he was dead. They had brought his limp body back to the settlement.

Eusebio walked over to the body and saw it was Se-eh-ha, the teenage boy who had given them water on their first morning. He knelt and prayed over the boy as the Pima people watched in sorrow.

"This must stop," Eusebio said angrily to Padre Aguilar. "This violence cannot continue."

The death disturbed Eusebio and Aguilar. In their anguish, they could not sleep, and stayed up talking. "What is this hatred some men have toward the native people?" Eusebio said. "It's as if the devil has entered their hearts."

"It is a base, uncivilized instinct that is unleashed here," Padre Aguilar said, shaking his head. "Obviously, they feel they will not be punished."

"I have given all my thought to the natives, but I see now we must do more to encourage the soldiers and ranch owners to come to our mass on Sundays," Eusebio said with new determination. "They have lost their Christianity. They have forgotten God."

Chapter Eight

A KINDRED SPIRIT

Once gossip began, it built to a crescendo, spreading from Mexico City to Guadalajara: Padre Eusebio Francisco Kino was too ambitious. He was starting too many missions, more than could be maintained, for his ego's sake. His only intention was to oversee more and more land. He provided help with crops and irrigation, but not enough Christian teaching.

Eusebio heard all these rumors. His fellow Jesuits were repeating—and believing—these absurd claims about him. He shook his head in disgust and remembered why he disliked the bureaucracy of the Jesuit order. The hierarchy brought out the worst in some of his Jesuit brothers and superiors. Were they simply envious that he was out in the desert, far from the restrictions they themselves struggled against?

One night he wrote to Father Ambrosio Oddón, the provincial of New Spain: "Send an official or come see for yourself who I am and what I am doing."

So he was not surprised when, on the afternoon of Christmas Eve, 1690, a visitor appeared, riding horseback toward Mission Dolores from across the plain. Eusebio came out of the small adobe barracks to watch the Jesuit approach.

"Padre Kino, I am Juan María de Salvatierra. I've just come from Guadalajara," the tall man said as he dismounted his horse. He wore a serious expression and a black cassock that was considerably cleaner than Eusebio's. His accent was distinctive. An Italian—and from the north!

"*Ciao e benvenuto!*" Eusebio greeted him with enthusiasm. It had been years since he'd spoken his own language, and he immediately warmed to the visitor, no matter what his intentions were.

The two men shook hands and Salvatierra asked to see the half-built church. He was charmed by it—the stones and adobe gave it a solid appearance, and inside the candlelight created a soft glow on the altar. Salvatierra suggested they conduct Christmas services there, and Eusebio enthusiastically agreed. That night, about fifty Pima men and women appeared, watching with reverence as the priests held mass.

The next morning, Eusebio and Salvatierra sat down to a hearty breakfast. Eusebio was eager to learn more about this man, so they launched into an intense discussion right away. Salvatierra was born in Milan, he explained, and studied at the Jesuit college in Parma. He was intrigued by what he'd read about indigenous people in New Spain, and after entering the Jesuit order in Genoa, he journeyed across the ocean to find them. Once there, he had lived among the Tarahumara tribe for ten years.

Eusebio soaked in these words from his fellow Italian—the two men clearly had much in common. Then Eusebio told his own story of growing up in the Italian Alps, studying in Germany, then coming here and gradually giving up his dream of going to China. He talked about his two years in Baja with Admiral Atondo, only to be forced to abandon his efforts at converting the willing people there.

"Baja! That is precisely where I want to go—and now you've shown me it is possible," Salvatierra said. His eyes lit up with excitement and he smiled at his new friend. "If I have to pay for all the expenses myself, I will. Depending upon others to fund our work just slows our progress."

"Well, before you go to Baja, I hope you will travel with me to visit all the missions in this region," Eusebio said. "You will see how we have been able to form good relationships with the people for many miles. They bring us their elders and their babies, asking us to baptize them."

Salvatierra shook his head. "As you know, I was sent to investigate the bad rumors and criticisms about you. But I suspect they were born out of envy of your success. If only they, and all missionaries, had your ability."

"Success . . ." Eusebio replied. "My friend, I have no success with the true challenge here." Salvatierra looked at him with interest. "I thought my missionary work was clear—to bring the gospel to innocent souls. But it is so much more complicated and difficult than that. The Pima—well, they are far more curious than dangerous. But the Spanish—their hatred and violence must be softened with God's truth and love. That is where I have been unsuccessful. They continue to terrorize tribes."

"But your missions are like mustard seeds—they will grow and transform this region and everyone in it," Salvatierra said. "And I want to see them! I have only your descriptions in my mind. I would like to visit them all."

"Very well," Eusebio said, his mood brightening again. "We will start tomorrow. We will ride a wide circuit and visit each of my missions. I will show you everything and introduce you to the caciques. We share a dream, my friend. With a few more Jesuit brothers, we can teach better methods of farming and raising cattle to people in the north and west, which will help the missions endure."

"The obstacles I see," Salvatierra said, "are the Spanish colonists, who destroy the trust we work so hard to build; the Apaches, who attack some weaker tribes; and our superiors in Mexico City, who are too far away to understand our needs."

Eusebio had yet to meet the Apaches, but he'd heard the Pima people refer to them with great uneasiness. He wondered how close they were to Mission Dolores. The two men began preparing for the first of their many journeys together as friends.

Chapter Nine

A BOAT IN THE DESERT

By now, Eusebio was adept in preparing for a new exploration of unknown regions. He knew how to calculate the number of men, horses, and mules needed for each adventure, as well as the amount of water and food. He noted the locations of water springs, rivers, and streams on his maps—each time he ventured out, he had more information to guide him.

He took Salvatierra across all the trails he had already established, impressing his new friend with the work he'd done at each fledgling mission. They were on their way back to Mission Dolores when three Pima men confronted them on the trail. Unsure of what the men wanted, Eusebio held up his hand to halt Salvatierra and their small group. But the three men surprised him by suddenly kneeling. Heads bowed, they begged the priests to visit their village several miles north.

"We must follow them," Eusebio said to Salvatierra, who nodded in agreement. They turned their horses northward.

Trailing the three Pima, they soon came upon the Santa Cruz River and a sprawling Pima *ranchería*. As men and women crowded around the Jesuits, Eusebio and Salvatierra got off their horses and tied them to a giant cottonwood tree. In the protection of the shade, the priests shared food and gifted the people small wooden crosses. They set up a little altar under the trees and baptized the infants brought to them by their mothers, praying for their long and prosperous lives. Several hours later, they departed.

"By now you have seen that with more missionaries here to help, so much more good could be done. By myself, I can only do a little," Eusebio said.

"You have my word, I will send more missionaries," Salvatierra said. "By divine grace, I shall try to be one of them."

As Salvatierra turned to leave, Kino noticed that his new friend's cassock was now as worn and dusty as his own.

The two men bid goodbye when they finally returned to Mission Dolores, but they both knew they would see each other again, and probably soon.

Inspired by his trip with Salvatierra, Eusebio embarked on another *entrada*, this time into the region of the lower Altar River. He took with him Padre Agustín de Campos, a twenty-four-year-old Spanish Jesuit priest who was painfully quiet, yet he watched Eusebio's missionary efforts carefully, hoping to learn from him.

The year was 1693. Campos had just told Eusebio terrible news: a massive earthquake and tsunami had occurred in

Sicily, destroying dozens of small towns. Eusebio reflected on life's brevity and fragility. Time was not to be wasted. He prayed for the people who died, and for those who survived in grief, for the long years of rebuilding to come. Then his mind wandered to Segno, the village in which he had lived with his parents in northern Italy. Suddenly, he longed to know—were they still alive? Or had one, or both, died? His heart ached.

His mind turned to his friend the duchess, and he prayed for her too. He sorely missed her wise counsel and conversation.

A movement at the end of the trail caught his eye. Eusebio looked up just in time to see three men of the Pima tribe's Soba faction bolt in terror at the sight of white men on horses. Even though he'd seen them only for a second, Eusebio wanted to see if they could be lured out with gifts and food. But these were lands in which Apaches often ventured, which meant he had to be cautious. And right now he did not have time to meet these Soba men.

Changing direction, Eusebio headed to the city of San Juan. He had an appointment with the General Domingo Jironza Pétriz de Cruzate, who controlled the Sonora region. He needed to request a military escort.

San Juan was a pleasant town with heavy-branched trees that provided pools of shade. Eusebio found the general easily; entering his official residence, Eusebio nodded deeply in respect. After polite introductions, the Jesuit made his request for a military man to accompany him into the Soba lands.

"Two Pima tribes have been at war for years," Eusebio said.

"I want to make peace between them—not just for their sake. It will expand the reach of Christian salvation and Spanish rule. But I do need military escorts. Can you provide a man or two who would be willing to travel long distances?"

General Jironza listened to the priest's request with a smile. "I have just the man for this adventure—my restless young nephew, Lieutenant Juan Mateo Manje. He recently arrived from Spain to help defend Spanish settlements against Apache attacks. He's here now—I will call him in so you can meet."

A strong, lean-muscled soldier entered the room and General Jironza asked him to sit. As he briefly described what Eusebio needed, the young lieutenant's eyes lit up.

"I have heard of you!" he said, turning to Eusebio.

"And what have you heard?" Eusebio asked. He liked the forthrightness of this young Spanish soldier with blond hair, but he wanted to know more about his character.

"That you are an effective missionary because you do not enslave the tribes nor force them to abandon their own religions. And by countering traditional missionary methods, you've converted more natives than nearly all other Jesuits in New Spain."

"Quite right," Eusebio said. "When you join me, I hope you will keep that approach in mind."

The two agreed to work together and immediately set out to equip their first journey into Soba lands. Eusebio quickly discovered that Manje was an intelligent and talkative travel companion who sought to learn everything he could from the natives. Unlike most Spanish soldiers, Manje viewed the Pima with curiosity—he had no desire to dominate them. He had taught himself several Pima languages and patiently taught Spanish to many native children. Eusebio was surprised to see how Manje enjoyed communicating with the Pima. He asked endless questions about how they hunted, cooked, and most importantly, how they chipped stones into fine-pointed arrows that were sharp enough to kill an animal—or a man.

The two men spent many days exploring regions to the northwest. Together, they discovered wide, fertile valleys, rocky mountains, and rushing rivers, which Eusebio carefully marked on his maps.

"It is easy to feel God in this wild country, don't you think?" Manje said when the two men took a rest during one trip. "The beauty of the landscapes and the open sky . . . All life here is immediate and inescapable."

"Yes, I agree," Eusebio said, surprised at the lieutenant's poetic comment. "Cutting wood for fires, hauling water from springs and streams, shooting deer for meat—living in this world requires strength and stamina. We must work hard simply to survive."

"Out here, I have freedom that I never felt in Spain," Manje said.

"I must admit," Eusebio said, "missionary work allows me a freedom too. When I was a boy, I needed to roam, to find God in my own way in the hills and valleys of my home. Natural landscapes were my childhood playgrounds. I grew up climbing hills and riding my horse across the Tyrol valleys."

"So exploration is your way of expressing love and faith in God?" Manje said, laughing.

"Yes, you could say so," Eusebio said. "I am compelled by the love and forgiveness bestowed upon me by Jesus to care for people in need. This is the work of all missionaries."

"But, Padre," Manje said, "how did you forsake women?"

"It is not that I gave up women," Eusebio said. "I do not dislike them, nor do I feel tempted by them. The love of God is simply bigger, far more important to me. And doing God's work in the world is the highest calling of all."

"I intend to marry one day," Manje said. "I love women and I want to have children—a large family. I hope to rise in the ranks of the military so I can give a wife and a family a prosperous life."

The men were quiet for a moment, then Manje added, "But I will put marriage off for as long as I can—I am not done exploring these regions!"

The two friends were equals in strength—neither balked at the sight of steep hills or deep streams. And they shared a longing to know and learn from the Pima people. Using gestures and a few learned Pima words, they did their best to convey respect and good will. At each new village they came upon, Eusebio talked to its curious inhabitants about creation and God, and he baptized children while Manje noted their numbers. They both asked about the peoples' use of plants for medicines, and the best trails for their journeys.

Venturing west, the two men scrambled up a rock-strewn peak named Cerro El Nazareno, which stood at the edge of a dry, sandy desert. At first they were confused about what they saw to the west, but then they shouted in surprise—gulf waters sparkled in the distance, and beyond that were the peaks of Baja mountains.

"The Spanish assume Baja is an island, but I believe it is a peninsula," Eusebio said. "God willing, one day I will prove it!"

"If only we could paddle across the gulf," Manje said.

Eusebio burst out laughing. "Why, you are right. We must build a boat! Truly, we could cross the gulf whenever we chose!"

That night, by the light of their campfire, they designed a boat that would be easy to sail and strong enough to withstand gulf's turbulent currents. The next day, they traveled to Caborca, where there grew plentiful cottonwood, mesquite, and pine trees they could cut down for their boat. They employed native and Spanish men to help. Padre Campos joined them and happily dove into the vigorous boat-building effort.

Manje tackled the work with enthusiasm and good humor. When one thick cottonwood tree refused to fall, he took the matter into his own hands. "Cut deep at the roots—that will make it fall!" he shouted. Padre Campos and the other men hacked, but still the tree would not fall.

"Stop—I know what to do," Manje said. He picked up a rope, climbed up on the tree trunk, and swung his body onto the nearest branch. As Eusebio and the other men watched in wonder, Manje shimmied up higher and higher. "I will tie the rope to a high branch, then we can use it to pull this tree down!" he shouted from the towering tree.

Suddenly, there was a loud crack—the tree was falling! Manje let go of the tree trunk just before it hit the ground. He rolled away from crashing branches, unscathed. He jumped up and laughed. "Well, there you see, God loves me!"

With great relief, Eusebio crossed himself and thanked God for the miracle that no one had been hurt. Then he had to laugh—even he would never take the risks Manje did.

An unexpected messenger arrived at Caborca early the next morning with a letter for Eusebio. The priest was fitting a long plank of timber into the side of the boat when he received the letter. He wiped his hands on his apron, then opened it.

The letter was from Padre Muñoz, his superior, who had written with an order: stop work on the boat immediately. Muñoz gave no reason, but Eusebio suspected that certain Jesuit priests simply wanted to restrict his freedom. He guessed someone thought building a boat to cross the gulf was foolish, or that Baja was not worth the effort to get there.

He sighed in frustration, then folded the letter and put it in his pocket. He surveyed the unfinished boat as dappled sunlight played across the rough wood. He saw Padre Campos working with tremendous focus as he adjusted a plank at the aft of the boat. He had a way of working that Eusebio appreciated—he paid attention to what was needed and then quietly did it. Campos demonstrated consistent loyalty to Eusebio and all that he tried to accomplish.

Eusebio wondered how he would tell Campos to stop building. What a waste—their progress had been so fast, and the men's workmanship was so skilled on the sturdy boat.

He had no choice. Like it or not, Eusebio was bound by a

vow of obedience, so he announced that the men's work must cease until further notice. They groaned and complained of this apparently arbitrary order.

Remaining idle was not an option. Eusebio decided to investigate a rumor about a vast abandoned dwelling along the Gila River, about 150 miles north from the half-built boat. The reverence with which his Pima friends talked about this place—it was a mixture of fear and awe—got his attention. He wanted to see what could have affected them so profoundly. To get there, he would pass by Bac, one of the largest Pima villages, and he was curious about that place too. Perhaps it was a good location for another mission.

Manje had come down with a fever from drinking dirty water and was too weak to get out to bed. Padre Campos agreed to stay and care for him, so Eusebio felt he could make the trip without his friend.

He called together his best guides and picked strong horses. It took five days of arduous travel through the hot desert to reach the place. At every chance, Eusebio stopped at villages along the way to meet people, learn about their customs, and bless them. Every encounter was a chance to bring a message of peace rather than fear.

"These nations are the Opas and Coco Maricopa," Eusebio wrote in his diary. Manje had been carefully noting how many people they met at each village—who knew how long it would be before other Europeans came to these remote regions? "They speak a language different from that of the Pima, though it is clear. As there were some who knew both languages well, I at once and with ease made a vocabulary of the tongue, and also a map of those lands, measuring the sun with an astrolabe."

The native languages had sounded like bird songs to him at first. But now that he could distinguish words, he tried to imitate them. The next day, at mid-morning, the Pima who led Eusebio's little caravan abruptly stopped their horses. The view ahead made them all sit up straight.

Eusebio shuddered. He did not believe in ghosts, except the Holy Ghost, but the sprawling group of buildings in the distance was eerily quiet, as if its residents were sleeping or had just left. An aqueduct indicated that the inhabitants had learned how to bring water from the river all the way to their dwelling.

Eusebio and his group approached slowly. The vast ruin of thick walls, which no longer had a roof, was four levels high and sat in the baking sun, completely empty of life. *How many people lived here—hundreds? Thousands?* Eusebio's mind tried to comprehend what he saw. *Clearly, they thrived for some time, but . . . what happened?*

The Pima guide who'd brought him here said one word: Hohokam. Eusebio asked for a translation: the people who vanished.

Eusebio named the place Casa Grande. That night, he wrote in his diary:

> *The Casa Grande is as large as a castle and equal to the largest church in these lands of Sonora. It is said that the ancestors of Montezuma deserted and depopulated it, and, beset by the*

neighboring Apaches, left for the east or Casas Grandes of Chi-huahua, and that from there they turned toward the south and southwest, finally founding the great city and court of Mexico. Close to this Casa Grande are thirteen smaller houses, some-what more dilapidated, and the ruins of many others, which make it evident that in ancient times there was a city here.

Pausing, he stared into the crackling campfire to think. *What about the families who lived there? Was their death caused by a drought or a disease? Was it the work of Apaches?* He wished he could have met the people, stayed with them, and learned about them. His heart filled with sadness. *They are beyond saving now*, he thought. *And their story is lost forever in the desert winds of time.*

His Pima companions offered no answers—they were super-stitious about the place and did not want to stay long. If the god Montezuma, who performed both good and evil deeds, had been involved here, they must be quiet and respectful. Eusebio watched as his Pima guides left arrows, feathers, and little gifts at the site of the Casa Grande to appease Montezuma.

Eusebio had no intention of dissuading them from their beliefs or offerings. They obviously had a need to understand—and avoid—whatever had devastated this large community of people, so like their own.

Chapter Ten

REVENGE

Danger lurked everywhere. Scorpions found their way into their sleeping quarters. More than once, Manje found one on the edge of his pillow as he got ready for bed. Rattlesnakes blended into the sand and would strike if disturbed. A soldier who accidentally stepped on one after taking off his boots died two days later. Coyotes yipped wildly at night when they killed their prey—a savage sound that set Eusebio's nerves on edge.

And then there was Lieutenant Antonio Solís. The Spanish military officer was charged with patrolling Spanish ranches and outposts, and he treated all men with disdain and suspicion. His violent temper was triggered by the slightest word or incident and, much to the concern of the priests, Solís kept his guns loaded and close by.

When two herds of horses were stolen from a mission in the Sonora region one night in the spring of 1694, the rumor was that the Sobaípuri were responsible. Taking a dozen Spanish soldiers with him, Lieutenant Solís armed himself and led the way to nearby villages. He noticed venison hanging to dry in one settlement and mistook it for meat of the stolen horses. Without warning, Solís shot and killed three Sobaípuri and captured several others before learning he'd retaliated against the wrong tribe.

Hearing about the incident the next day, Eusebio was furious. He quickly assembled a small group to accompany him to the village where it had taken place, hoping to ease tensions. But before they got there, he received more bad news. Another Spanish officer, under the pretense of quashing a revolt, plundered a village north of Mission Dolores, killing all the Pima men and taking the women and children as slaves for his friend's ranch. Eusebio listened to the news in horror, sickened and angry that these men could be so ruthless and inhumane. He noted the officer's name and vowed never to forget it.

These incidents led to tribal warriors ambushing Spanish settlements, then subsequent counterattacks, many with Lieutenant Solís in command. Until this time, men of the Pima supported the Spanish and fought as allies against other tribes, but they retaliated when their own tribes were attacked.

To make matters worse, a group of over two hundred Apaches were ambushed just before launching a coordinated attack against a Spanish settlement. The Apaches had horses, which gave them strategic advantage in a fight, but the Pima fought with poison arrows.

Eusebio grieved at each news of escalating violence—he knew some of the victims, including people he'd baptized. *All our work to establish trust is being destroyed, perhaps forever!* he thought. *Why do Solís or the other officers not consult me about matters before killing people?* He prayed for courage and for help. He prayed for peace.

But when he finally met Solís face-to-face in an abandoned Pima village, he shook with anger. "You must stop these attacks!" he shouted. "You assume they are your enemies, or that you can do what you want to them. But in the name of God, you cannot. You must not shoot."

While Eusebio glared at him, Solís sat on his horse and looked down at the priest as if he were a rattlesnake. It was not a Christian thought, he knew, but Eusebio hated Solís for killing the very people he had dedicated his life to save.

Solís shrugged at the priest's outburst. His dark, dissolute face told the story of his character. He was a crude man. He might have been handsome as a young soldier, but bitterness had made him ugly. He had no need for priests; he would do what he wanted. His own men feared him.

"Our mission, *on order from the crown*, is to bring Christian morality to these regions. These killings put our mission, and all our priests, in danger," Eusebio said. He stood just a few feet from the lieutenant, who had not only a gun but also a sharp sword at his belt. The two men scowled at each other. Sun beat on their faces and sweat prickled their necks.

"Padre, I defend our people and our property," Solís said, as if explaining to a child. "We cannot have revolts. If mistakes are made—well, that is the cost of their crimes against us and against the crown."

"What crimes?" Eusebio said. "I know them and they know

me. Honest dealings will make us all safer—far safer than killing innocent people. Let me negotiate with them before you use your guns." With this, he turned to head back to Mission Dolores.

"Padre, where are you? Wake up!" a deep voice bellowed outside as Eusebio slept soundly. Then the sound of his door crashing finally woke him from his dreams. It was just before dawn, he could tell by the dim light. He jumped out of bed and nearly ran into Solís, who stood in the middle of his room. The lieutenant's eyes blazed with anger.

"They've taken my wife and my daughter!" he spat. "These people you care so much about—they are kidnappers and murderers! If you know anything about this, tell me where they are!"

Eusebio was taken aback. "No, of course I do not know! I don't understand."

"I awoke just ten minutes ago and found my wife missing, and my daughter too. It's the Pima—this is their revenge. Get dressed, Padre. You are going to help me find them!"

"I will get my horse and meet you by the river," Eusebio said. He quickly put on his clothes and boots and ran outside. At the river, Solís had already gathered some of his men. As the rising sun cast its pink glow on the hills, he ordered the men to go in several directions toward the *rancherías*.

"No firing of weapons, please!" Eusebio pleaded. But Solís would not agree.

After riding for forty-five minutes, Eusebio stopped by a stream so his horse could drink. He dismounted and scanned the landscape. It was so unlikely that any Pima would kidnap two Spanish women, no matter how much they hated Solís. He'd never known them to kidnap anyone before. What could have happened?

At the sound of a loud splash, he turned to see a teenage girl climb out of the stream, soaking wet. An older woman at the edge pulled her out, scolding her for being clumsy.

"Señora!" Eusebio called. The woman looked up, her eyes wide with fear as she clutched the thin, shivering girl. He knew at once he'd found the wife and daughter of Antonio Solís.

"Padre—" she began. Eusebio ran to give her a hand up the embankment to where his horse was tied.

"Señora, what has happened? Your husband is looking for you."

"He can't find us. Please . . . Padre, he is a bad man." She pulled her daughter close. The two women looked cold and weak. "You might have seen his temper. We have been the recipients of his rage for too long, and he is strong." She dropped her eyes, and Eusebio noticed her nose was unnaturally crooked— had it been broken?

Speechless, Eusebio sought a comforting response. "I will not tell him. I will make sure he does not find you."

"He was drunk last night, so I thought we could finally escape. He has hit us many times, and last night he threw a chair at my daughter. I knew then that we had to leave—though I have no plan, no place to go. I just need to be away from him." As she looked out into the desert, Eusebio started thinking what he could do.

"How did you escape?" he asked, then he noticed a mule under the tree.

"That was the only animal I could get without trouble," she said, gesturing to the mule.

"I will need to get you to Guadalajara, then perhaps to Mexico City," Eusebio said. "I know people there who can help you. But we must be fast—your husband has gone in the opposite direction from here. If we get back to Mission Dolores right now, then tomorrow morning you can escape in the darkness. Are you strong enough to ride on my horse?"

"Yes, I am—we are," the woman said. Eusebio helped the two women climb up behind him on his horse. They trotted quietly back down to Mission Dolores. There, Eusebio hid the woman and her daughter in his own office, then climbed his horse and took off again, pretending he'd seen nothing.

True to his word, Padre Salvatierra arranged for a young Jesuit priest to join Eusebio at Mission Dolores. His name was Padre Francisco Xavier Saeta and he had recently arrived from Sicily.

Eusebio greeted him when he arrived on horseback. "*Benvenuto, fratello!*" he said, shaking the young priest's hand. "Come, please stay until you've gotten your bearings." He was excited for another Italian to be in the region.

"Thank you. I happily accept your offer," the young man said. "I have admired your work from afar and am honored to meet you—and learn from you!"

"And I will share all I know to help you begin your mission here," Eusebio said. He liked this young, cheerful man who exuded a positive energy—the very thing Eusebio realized he'd lost.

"Padre Kino, before we speak of anything further, I've brought you a message," Saeta said. Eusebio looked at him quizzically. "It's not a written note, but a message from the wife of Lieutenant Antonio Solís. I met her in Mexico City, where she is staying at the home of a nun, who is also a poet. This wife wants you to know she and her daughter are safe. And she thanks you for saving their lives."

Eusebio flushed red. He was happy and relieved to receive this news, but obviously Padre Saeta now knew he had deceived a Spanish officer concerning his wife's whereabouts. This would not be acceptable to his Jesuit superiors—they would severely reprimand him if they found out.

"I will tell no one about this message, in case you are worried," the young priest said solemnly. "I understand the circumstances of her departure."

"It was difficult," Eusebio said, grateful Saeta was a man of discretion. "Her husband is a violent man who has killed many people here and made our work harder than it should be. After searching every settlement of native people in this region, he finally gave up, and though he would not admit it, he knew she had left on her own. He did not seem to care whether she died in the desert."

After touring the region with Eusebio, Padre Saeta wrote to the superiors in Mexico City for permission to begin a new mission in Caborca, near the Altar River. In reality, he had already started it before he got their approval; he named it Mission Nuestra Señora de la Concepción del Caborca.

Eusebio generously brought cattle, horses, food, and crop seeds to Caborca, and provided servants and herdsmen. Saeta set about organizing his new mission and traveling to neighboring Pima villages to introduce himself to the caciques and to distribute gifts.

Eusebio had great hopes for this new outpost and he enjoyed Saeta's energy, yet he was also uneasy. Caborca was close to the tribes who had been retaliating against the Spanish. When he finally mentioned his worries to the young priest, Saeta dismissed the danger. With charming confidence, he assured Eusebio and his friend Lieutenant Juan Manje that making peace with the native tribes was his priority. He visited Mission Dolores often for Padre Kino's wise counsel on matters of agriculture and raising cattle, and when he could not visit, he sent letters that reported his mission's crops were growing well.

"A herdsman has built a corral for the horses you provided," he wrote, "and he is now building a larger residence. I hope to bring more Jesuit priests to Mission Caborca. I am, as always, optimistic about our success."

Eusebio and Manje were pleased to receive these reports. They felt as if they'd gained a younger brother, and they were eager to see how his mission would grow.

Spring in the Sonoran Desert was more colorful than Padre Saeta ever expected. Sienna-colored rabbitbrush dotted the landscape and dark green piñon trees stood like soldiers. Juniper trees, with their twisted trunks, provided plenty of shade and the saguaro cacti sprouted white flowers.

Now Padre Saeta dug in the dirt next to the chapel while humming a German hymn he'd known since he was a child—it calmed his churning mind. Several days before, he had heard a disturbing story of two Spanish military men who'd come upon women of the Jocome tribe washing in the river. They'd raped two of the women and carried off a third. The following day, a group of Jocome men attacked a Spanish ranch and stole ten horses. He shook his head in frustration, thinking, *These attacks can be prevented. I have come here at just the right time to bring peace.*

It was April 2, 1695. A recent rain had made the desert soil as soft as it would ever be for the garden he intended to plant.

Then a heavy clop of approaching horses made Saeta turn and stand quickly. About ten men from Tubutama, Oqui-toa, and Pitquín tribes, all carrying bows and arrows, approached on horseback. The leader, a tall, young Tubutama man, whose long hair was pulled back by a leather thread, stared silently at Saeta.

Saeta returned his gaze and smiled, but he was afraid. He tried to gauge the men's mood. They had ridden toward him too quickly. Their eyes did not look peaceful, but rather set and angry. A prickly sensation electrified Saeta's skin.

Abruptly, the leader and six of his men drew their bows and arrows, aiming at the priest.

Saeta raised his hands. "No, do not kill me," he begged, his voice choking. "Believe me, I am here in peace."

At one short word from the leader, the men released their arrows, shooting deep into the padre's chest. He staggered backward, stumbling into the small chapel. The men dismounted their horses and followed him. As Saeta fell toward the simple wooden altar, he wrapped his arms around a crucifix that stood on a table. At close range, the men shot more arrows into him. He slumped sideways to the ground, dark blood spilling from his wounds.

Hearing the commotion, his servants ran out of the mission to see their fallen padre in the chapel. Arrows pierced them too, and they fell, pools of their blood mingling in the blazing afternoon sunlight. The killers returned to their horses and galloped away.

A young Pima man rode through the early morning desert on his horse, his long hair flying back from his face. The cool stillness before sunrise was ideal for fast travel. A few jackrabbits darted away from his speeding horse, but mostly he saw no other movement.

He knew the way to the Mission Dolores, about one hundred miles away. He had been baptized by the kind padre there. But he had never ridden the distance at this speed.

He had to alert Padre Kino about the death of his friend. All the priests must know—they were in danger.

A sharp slice of sunlight peeked up over the distant blue mountain as the rider galloped on his horse, carrying his terrible news.

~

After receiving the news, Lieutenant Manje offered to go to Caborca to retrieve Padre Saeta's body and what was left of his belongings. Eusebio, in shock at the news of his friend's death, sat on a rough bench outside the chapel. "Yes, go, as soon as you can," he said, nodding. Manje, pained with sorrow, strode off to ready his horse for departure.

Eusebio's mind reeled with grief and disbelief. He pictured Saeta's kind face, his enthusiastic smile and talk about the mission's future, and his desire to bring as many people as possible into the loving fold of Christianity.

He had to get away and walk in the wilderness. Eusebio followed the trail that led to a small ridge near the mission. It was afternoon and still hot, but he was too disturbed to rest indoors.

Ever since blood was first shed months before, it seemed to spread like a disease. Eusebio blamed Solís, but he was just one of many Spanish military men who killed with impunity. So many of them were ruthless and cruel toward the native people. What happened to them—how had they lost all humanity?

Eusebio considered young Saeta as a martyr. *He came to do God's work and he was killed*, he thought. *We all suffer as missionaries, but most of us suffer for long hours every day, years at time. His was the ultimate sacrifice—a sudden, bloody death.*

To Eusebio, Saeta embodied the true missionary spirit. He brought joy and optimism to this place. He cared about justice. He planted seeds that grew into abundant produce, which he shared with the nearby tribes. He was innocent and welcoming, which made him an easy target for a revenge attack in this dry, dusty land.

Eusebio wept on a boulder, his head in his hands. Never had he felt so hopeless. Had he put Saeta in danger by not warning him more forcefully about the threat around him? Would he ever be able to stem this violence from all sides? The young priest embodied real hope for this land, these people, and their future—and the Jesuits' chance to bring peace.

Now Saeta was dead. *Is it just a matter of time before this is my fate too? Am I like Jesus, facing my Jerusalem?*

Eusebio stopped crying and lifted his head. The superiors in Mexico City might very well use Saeta's death as a reason to withdraw all Jesuits from these regions. And they had no idea what instigated these attacks, that it was the relentless violence of the Spanish military and landowners against the tribes.

To honor Saeta and all the natives who had been peacefully and willingly baptized, Eusebio decided he must inform his superiors and the viceroy of New Spain of the truth. He would go to Mexico City—or Madrid, or even Rome if he had to—to report the crimes against the tribes' men and women by Solís and other officers of the army.

But before that, he had one more critical task to do.

Eusebio sent word to all the caciques of nearby settlements and to Spanish officers, including Solís. He wanted to resolve the tension that made everyone wary and afraid. He asked that Padre Saeta's killers come forward for punishment by their own tribes, and that a peace agreement be forged by all sides. No weapons would be permitted at this gathering.

He was pleased when all parties agreed to arrive at the designated date for this rare peace meeting. The first group of men to arrive were from several tribes, and as agreed, they placed their bows and arrows beneath a grove of mesquite trees at a distance, then sat and waited.

Eusebio, accompanied by Lieutenant Juan Manje, arrived within hours and sat with the tribesmen. In the distance they saw a cloud of dust—Spanish soldiers were approaching on horseback. The soldiers drew close, but remained on their horses. This bothered Eusebio—it was a deliberate refusal to participate as equals with the others. Nevertheless, he began by asking for the guilty Pima men to identify themselves. Four young men slowly stood with their heads bowed as their elders watched sternly. As Eusebio spoke, a soldier jumped off his horse and attempted to tie the hands of the one of the young men as if to take him away.

"Stop! What are you doing?" Eusebio demanded.

Suddenly, fearing a trap, the Pima men jumped to their feet and backed away.

"This is one of the murderers!" the soldier said, grabbing the young Pima man by the hair and jerking his head back.

In a flash, Solís stepped forward, drew his sword, and beheaded the young man. Blood gushed out of his body as the others began shouting and running in every direction. Eusebio cried out and the Pima raced to their bows and arrows. Soldiers chased them on horseback, trampling some and shooting others.

Eusebio helplessly watched, then ran to the fallen men, administering last rites when he could.

In thirty minutes, those who could run away had disappeared. Stunned by the horror he had witnessed, Eusebio walked among the dead, tears streaming down his face. He could hardly breathe, he was so angry and distraught. Forty-eight men lay dead on the ground, among them men from several tribes and three soldiers.

At the edge of the gruesome scene, he turned and kneeled on the dry ground.

Father Almighty, please hold these souls in your loving hands, he prayed. He opened his eyes to survey the bodies around him. *This place will be called La Matanza—the slaughter. No one must forget how peace was betrayed.*

Two days later, Juan María de Salvatierra visited Eusebio at Mission Dolores. The old friends immediately embraced.

"I came as soon as I heard about the death of Padre Saeta," Salvatierra said. "And I just learned you've had more deaths. I am devastated."

"Yes, it is a terrible time," Eusebio said as he invited him inside for a meal. Salvatierra noticed his friend looked uncharacteristically pale and ill. "I am glad to see you. It seems the Spanish ignore all we try to do, and they believe no law governs their behavior—so they kill whomever they choose."

"God help them," Salvatierra said. His dark eyes were filled with sorrow. He admired Eusebio's consistent courage and determination and wondered if that would be enough to carry him through this dangerous time.

"I have made a decision," Eusebio said as the two men sat at a heavy wooden table to eat food the servants brought out.

Salvatierra kept his eyes on his friend. What was he about to do? "I must go to Mexico City," Eusebio continued, "to tell our superiors—and the viceroy—about the cruel acts of the Spanish army that led to these attacks. I know it's a long journey—perhaps fifteen hundred miles—and it will take me away from here at a time when I could prevent further attacks. But I must report the names of those men who have done the worst crimes against the Pima and other tribes. If I do not tell the truth to those in power, they will believe the tribes are attacking for no reason."

"I will go too," Salvatierra said.

"We will have to wait for the weather to cool," Eusebio said. The two men began discussing the supplies they would need and the best routes to take.

That night, Eusebio put pen to paper. He wrote down every injustice against the tribes by Spanish men that he had witnessed or heard about. He noted the date and place of each incident, how each one began, and how many people were killed, injured, or enslaved as a result. And he recorded the names of every Spanish officer he knew who had taken part in killing or acts of violence against innocent people.

Hours later, he put down his pen and reviewed the document. As far as he knew, it was complete.

Then he had another idea. He would write a book about Padre Francisco Xavier Saeta, and his life and work in the Pimería Alta. No one should forget that cheerful spirit who lost his life doing God's work.

Eusebio's journey took seven weeks. After giving the Christmas Eve mass in the candlelit mission at Guadalajara—a holy experience that revived his spirit—Eusebio arrived in Mexico City on January 8, 1696. He brought with him two Pima boys who were willing to testify that many Pima families remained devoted to the Jesuits, who had helped improve their lives. They wanted to tell the stories of two vicious attacks by the Spanish soldiers that killed ten of their family members.

Eusebio wasted no time in setting an appointment with the Jesuit leaders and the viceroy. After being ushered into their chambers, Eusebio sat before the men—the new provincial named Padre Juan de Palacios, the viceroy, and several other dignitaries. Eusebio certainly looked like a different man from the one who'd arrived from Italy fifteen years before. His hair was long and unkempt. Wild, dark curls fell over his collar. He was just fifty years old, but his skin was rough and lined from years in the sun. Wrinkles around his eyes made him look more like an old rancher than a priest.

The Jesuit leaders remembered when he'd arrived—a refined, well-educated Italian priest who exuded an uncommon energy and passion. He still had that same energy, but nothing about him seemed refined anymore. He had become a man of the desert—a little wild and certainly unpredictable. Most priests were satisfied to be left alone in their routines, but Eusebio was just the opposite. He had always embraced the Sonoran Desert's rough terrain and purposely spent his life among the natives, whose customs and language seemed so alien to others.

The older men politely listened to him speak, but Eusebio sensed their skepticism. His presence made them uncomfortable. They were probably thinking of the rumors about him that continued to circulate: he disobeyed the rules; he only wanted power, to rule over more and more land.

But they were riveted by Eusebio's vivid, detailed accounts of the atrocities committed by Spanish officers against innocent Pima people, and his claims that the uprisings were the direct result. Eusebio made his case convincingly, naming the guilty men and suggesting harsh punishment. Although he defended the Pima's actions, of course, a few of them had committed atrocities such as Padre Saeta's murder. But in his experience, he attested, most tribes had a strong morality and were not violent. Salvatierra concurred with Eusebio's accounts.

As Salvatierra spoke, Eusebio noticed the viceroy's wife slip into the room. A middle-aged woman with a warm smile, she delighted in meeting the Pima boys at the side of the room. Eusebio was struck by her dark blue dress—the fabric was clean and fine compared to the rough pieces of leather and fur native women wore.

The sight of her stirred in him sad feelings—he suddenly wished he could see his friend the duchess. He missed their intimate conversations. Would he ever see her again? It pained him to think the answer was no.

He turned his attention back to the proceedings. The Pima boys were asked to share their stories. As they described how they'd seen their family shot and killed by Spanish officers, the viceroy's wife dabbed tears from her eyes with a lace handkerchief.

When the meeting ended, Eusebio stood and said, "Let the blood of Padre Saeta be a nourishment to the soil, from which may spring up and grow a strong Christian community. I can think of nothing our dear padre would have wanted more."

He requested at least five more Jesuit priests be sent to Mission Dolores and the surrounding missions to help reestablish peace. In the end, the officials agreed to nearly all his requests.

After a month in Mexico City, he and Salvatierra began the long journey back to the Pimería. The viceroy insisted three military men accompany Eusebio and Salvatierra on their way home; the priests reluctantly agreed. The group traveled northward slowly and mostly in the late afternoons, stopping often at water springs to keep their horses and mules refreshed.

Eusebio wished he felt better about his meeting in Mexico City. Did it really matter that he'd told them about the violence perpetrated by the Spanish army? What can they do about it? *Maybe God is the only one who can stop that kind of violence*, he thought.

After cresting a small hill, Eusebio recognized that they had entered the land of Jocome tribes. At a resting stop, he suggested to Salvatierra that they pay a short visit to three Jesuit priests who worked in a nearby mission. Attacks had recently taken place here and he wanted to make sure they were safe.

After assuring the Spanish soldiers that he and Salvatierra would be gone for just a few hours, they left to find their Jesuit friends. The soldiers were happy to take a break and agreed to wait for the priests under a grove of ironwood trees beside a stream.

Two hours later, Eusebio and Salvatierra returned in good spirits—their friends were not only safe but had treated them to a fine lunch.

But they stopped short as they approached the ironwood trees. The bloody bodies of the Spanish soldiers lay sprawled on the ground, pierced with arrows of the Jocome tribe.

Nauseous and distraught, Eusebio and Salvatierra knelt and prayed over the dead soldiers. They had no choice but to continue a grim march onward to Mission Dolores, but they kept their eyes trained on the horizon at all times, nervously watching for signs of trouble.

It was May of 1696 when the cacique named Coxi received word that his revered old friends Eusebio and Salvatierra were about to arrive back in the Pimería from Mexico City. He called for all his people to gather in full celebratory dress at the mission to greet the priests with drums. As the two exhausted Jesuits returned, their hearts leapt at the cheerful reception. They were gratified to be met with such a warm welcome.

Eusebio stood on a small box and spoke to the crowd in the Pima language. By now he was fluent. He thanked them for their presence at Mission Dolores and for their faith and loyalty. After conveying good wishes from the viceroy and other officials in Mexico City, he said, "May peace be with you."

For the next two weeks, the Pima helped the padres harvest the bushy yellow wheat that now grew abundantly in the fields surrounding the mission. At the end of the harvest, Eusebio once again called for a great peace gathering at Mission Dolores. He invited Pima chiefs, Spanish military men, and Jesuit missionaries. After mass, Eusebio encouraged each group to offer a few conciliatory words.

One by one, each man stepped forward to express sorrow for past violence and to promise to live in peace. The Pima cacique sang a song, then the men silently stood in a large circle. A warm breeze rustled the leaves above.

"'Love the Lord your God with all your heart and with all your soul and with all your mind and with all your strength,'" Eusebio said, quoting his favorite passage from the Bible. "'Love your neighbor as yourself.' May we all live by these commandments."

He closed his eyes. The breeze was the Holy Ghost's blessing of this sacred gathering. These men had many differences, but for this one precious moment they were joined in a desire for a peace that would last.

Chapter Eleven

NEW ORDERS

Schools of little fish darted past him in cool blue water. Kelp waved in front of his face, but he maneuvered around it, over bright orange coral. Eusebio sensed he had to reach a designated spot very soon, though he wasn't sure why. A woman's wavering voice sang a wordless song—was it the duchess?

Eusebio kicked his feet to accelerate. He enjoyed this feeling of power in the water—in fact, it comforted him. He just couldn't go fast enough.

"Padre, Padre!" a voice cut through the deep water. Eusebio started and awoke from his dream. A young Pima boy shook his shoulders. "Time to get up, Padre! A man has come with a letter for you."

As usual, Eusebio had not slept in a bed, but on two pieces of cowhide beneath a tree, covered by a wool blanket. For a pillow, he propped up his saddle.

His Jesuit brothers had long wondered why he slept outside. Eusebio did not bother to explain. He was deeply comforted by staring at the constellations as he went to sleep. They were like a perfect otherworld that awakened his imagination. He studied them until his eyes closed. And there was another reason: He wanted to live as Pima did, the people among whom he lived and served. He wanted to feel close to the earth, to notice and learn all of nature's rhythms.

But he'd been having dreams recently in which he was being called to another place far away from Mission Dolores—he wondered if that place was Baja. He often thought about the men, women, and children he'd baptized there, how poor yet friendly they had been—and how badly they were treated by Admiral Atondo and his men. He'd always regretted leaving.

The tantalizing smell of food wafted from the mission kitchen. He rose to get water to wash his face and hands, passing the little church with seven bells, the blacksmith's workshop, the carpenter's workshop, and the water-powered mill. In the distance, he could see the mission's fruit tree orchards, a vineyard, and a winery. Herds of cattle were raised here, and Eusebio personally drove them to missions in distant valleys. Mission Dolores was thriving under his direction.

As he walked to get breakfast, he reflected on his dream. He and Salvatierra repeatedly requested permission to go to Baja, but their Jesuit superiors continued saying no. His work in the Pimería was far too important, they said. His presence was critical to that region's enduring peace.

"Padre, the letter!" The little boy who had woken him called, standing beside a Spanish officer who had just arrived from Guadalajara.

Eusebio strode over, offered the man breakfast, and took the letter. It was from Padre Juan de Palacios. Eusebio had been reassigned to Baja, California, so he could revitalize the old missions and start new ones with Padre Juan Salvatierra.

Eusebio's heart was torn—he longed return to Baja, yet he'd built Mission Dolores with his own hands. He knew and trusted the Pima people around him, and they trusted him. He shared with them everything he knew about growing crops and livestock, and the Pima people shared their abundant crops with him. He no longer saw them as different or strange—they were, in essence, his family. He knew their names and their children. He prayed for and blessed them. But he had to go if this is what he was ordered to do.

Some of Eusebio's Jesuit superiors in Mexico City were against this order too, considering the high number of missions he had established and how well they thrived under his direction. And the news did not sit well with the Pima people. Without him, they felt unprotected from the violence of Spanish soldiers.

Three days into his journey toward the coast, Eusebio was overtaken by a courier on horseback who carried a message from Mexico City. The new assignment was revoked. Eusebio was to return to the Pimería to uphold peace.

The message also said Eusebio did have permission—indeed, he was encouraged—to explore Baja and other regions. But his base must always be Mission Dolores.

Salvatierra, however, had permission to continue to Baja

and revive the missions that had been built years before. Euse-bio laughed. Why had it taken his superiors so long to see this solution?

By the time he reached Cósari, Eusebio had come to terms with this new order; he'd been given the best of all worlds. His beloved Mission Dolores would remain his home, from which he could plan more expeditions, and even revisit Baja.

He was not the only happy one. Pima people and caciques wearing colorful clothing decorated with beads and feathers danced in the village of Cósari. They beat sticks and drums in celebration of Padre Kino's return.

Eusebio had returned with the company of Padre Horacio Polici, who had joined him along the route to see for himself what the famous Jesuit had built. Padre Polici was a cynical old man who viewed Eusebio with skepticism. He knew the rumors that Eusebio had exaggerated his achievements and that he ignored newly arrived young missionaries by going on too many adventures—rumors that were wiped from his mind at the sight of this enthusiastic crowd.

Eusebio got off of his horse and spoke to the Pima people gathered in front of the mission. After introducing them to the honored and important guest, Padre Polici, the celebrants per-formed an elaborate dance with song and beating drums.

In spite of his pessimism, Padre Polici was flattered at this extravagant display of loyalty and support. He'd never been cheered by a crowd in his entire life. Before departing, he prom-ised to send more missionaries to help Eusebio expand his missionary reach. He was won over.

Chapter Twelve

PUSHING WEST

"Do you pray?" Eusebio asked Lieutenant Manje as they sat next to a campfire. They had been traveling for days and were both tired.

"Yes . . . well, no," Manje stammered. "Not as much as I should."

"Even a little prayer from time to time can bring you closer to God, and God closer to you," he said. He smiled, but Manje avoided his eyes.

"But often, I just . . . don't believe," Manje said. "I cannot pray, then."

"I wonder about the strength of my own faith sometimes," Eusebio confessed. "Still, I pray. I pray for my faith to be stronger and for God to give me courage to go on, even when my faith is weak."

"You admit weakness to God? I admire you, my friend."

"Yes, God is loving, no matter how devoted we are."

"I've never met a padre who talks this way," Manje laughed. "Most of them are rule makers and rule followers."

"We need priests in these lands who can be much more than that, wouldn't you say?" Eusebio asked, gesturing to the night desert, illuminated by moonlight.

"Indeed, we do," Manje replied as the two men began preparing their pallets for sleep.

They awoke just before sunrise on an early November morning in 1697 to travel as far as they could before the heat became unbearable.

A soldier, Lieutenant Cristóbal Martín Bernal joined them at the outset. He was sent, he said, to verify Eusebio's claims that all Pima tribes were friendly toward the Spanish. Though the Pima had attacked some missions, Eusebio pointed out that these were in retaliation after Spanish military had killed dozens of their people. The attacks ended after Eusebio had visited the caciques in each Pima region.

Now Eusebio's goal was to explore lands further west—first to a great *ranchería* called Quíburi that was strategically located on a high bluff, just on the edge of Apache lands. This was the home of a Pima tribe called Sobaípuri whose cacique was Coro, a highly respected leader among all Pima tribes. Eusebio was eager to meet him, but he, Manje, and Bernal were unprepared for what they found when they reached Quíburi.

There, a crowd of Sobaípuri warmly greeted and led the

visitors directly to Chief Coro, who smiled and appeared welcoming. But the travelers quickly realized they had interrupted a celebration. As they walked into the center of the village, they stopped. In the middle of a wide open space stood a pole onto which were nailed the scalps of fifteen men.

Sobaípuri men beat drums as women danced in a circle around the pole. Through an interpreter, Eusebio learned the scalps were from Jocome and Janos warriors from Apache tribes—sworn enemies of the Sobaípuri.

The visitors were invited to join in their latest triumphant victory over the enemies, and to eat, drink, and dance. Happy to be offered a drink and a reason to celebrate, Bernal and Manje unbuttoned their dusty jackets and tried to imitate the dancers, making everyone laugh.

Eusebio did not join them. He held back, trying to hide his revulsion at the sight of the scalps and the open display of bloodlust. He understood their euphoria—Apache tribes were ruthless raiders. But as a Jesuit and a man of peace, Eusebio could not revel in a bloody victory.

"We must stay here for a few days," Eusebio told Manje and Bernal that night. "It would be an insult to Chief Coro if we left this celebration sooner. Our alliance with him is important. We—and the Spanish army—need him as our ally."

"I don't mind—it is comfortable here and these people are good," Manje said, unrolling his sleeping mat.

Lieutenant Bernal was quiet, thinking. Eusebio wondered if the soldier was still suspicious of their hosts. "This has been a revelation," Bernal finally said. "I see now that we are not their enemy and they are not ours. I admire Chief Coro, and it's clear the tribes' histories have intertwined allegiances and conflicts, long before we arrived in these lands. I'm glad you allowed me to travel with you, Padre. You are right—we need Coro on our side. I plan to tell the other officers about him."

Eusebio thanked God for Bernal's presence. If there were a way to stop the Spanish army's violence, many peaceful meetings like this one would have to take place.

As he did every night, Eusebio prayed to be an instrument of God's peace—among the native people and the Spanish—while he scanned the heavens for familiar constellations. Then he fell into a deep sleep.

After departing the Quíburi settlement a few days later, Lieutenant Bernal left Eusebio and Manje to continue visiting Sobaípuri villages on his own.

Now Eusebio, Manje, and a dozen servants and guides kept going. With plenty of water and supplies, they were full of confidence. But when they arrived at the edge of a strikingly barren, arid desert, their morale began to waver. This was known to be a treacherous crossing, their guides said, yet there was no way around it. Luckily, it was February, the coolest month to cross.

"Have you heard of this crossing?" Manje asked Eusebio. They stood on a small rocky mound that looked out over the flat expanse of yellow-white sand. The landscape was dotted by the slender stalks of a few ocotillo cacti and upright saguaro.

"It will be difficult, yes. We can only travel in the late afternoon and at night to avoid the sun," Eusebio said.

"Men die here," Manje said grimly. "They never reach the other side."

"We are prepared," Eusebio said. He sounded confident, but a flutter of fear in his chest made him take a deep breath. In fact, *many* men had died on this passage—he heard the guides talk about it.

They began the next evening, aiming to reach a water tank or small natural reservoir known to be located several hours away. The moon rose, blanketing the flat landscape with a bright white light to illuminate the way across a faint trail.

As the group silently progressed, Eusebio experienced a strange sense of dislocation. They passed no houses and no human beings, only a few jackrabbits. He had no sense of time, where he'd come from, or where he was going. The rhythm of their horses' and mules' hooves softly plodding was like the beating of his own heart, reminding him of the beating drums of Coxi's tribe. All he knew was that the moon was somehow pulling him in the right direction.

Eusebio shook himself—he'd been dozing in the saddle.

"Where is the water?" Manje angrily asked the guides. They said they somehow must have passed it. "The animals need water—*we* need water!" Manje was exasperated.

Eusebio realized they were in danger. Another water tank could be found further on, the guides said—they were positive. The group had no choice but to push on.

Finally, long after midnight, they reached a deep gorge. The guides slid off their horses and found a steep, rocky path up to a hidden pool of water, fed by a deep spring. "Let's call this place Moon Tank," Manje said, drinking deeply.

After everyone was sated, they set up to sleep under a small cliff. Eusebio fell asleep almost instantly after lying down under his blanket. In his dreams, he met his friend, Duchess de Aveiro. She was radiant, happy, and out of breath. She looked younger than when he'd last seen her in Spain.

"I've run all the way from Seville!" she said, laughing and gathering up the skirts of her dress to sit on a large boulder near the Moon Tank.

"How is Seville? And how are you? You have not written to me in years," Eusebio said.

"I am sorry. I have missed you, even though I have not sent letters. Seville is prospering again after so much death and disease," the duchess said. "When I see Jesuit priests on the street, I always hope you will be among them and you will come to my house again so we can talk about the stars or theology."

"I miss our conversations also," Eusebio said. "My life here . . . it's hard. I came to convert the natives, and I've found these tribes to be strong and spiritual—they have their own way of praying, and of course many gods. My wish is to lead them to our God with a gentle hand, but I also need to soften the hearts of the Spanish. I am losing hope that my work will ever reach enough people."

"God supports you, not the Spanish," the duchess said sharply. "And God will reward you. Look, I will travel with you and remind you of the great good you are doing. You've come so far. You are not just a missionary; you are a brave pioneer. Let me see—which horse can I ride?"

Eusebio lurched awake, looking for a horse for the duchess. He realized sadly that he'd been dreaming.

A faint hint of light edged up at the horizon. He rubbed his eyes and smiled. It was as if she'd been here. He took a deep breath, put his head back on the ground, and slept peacefully for another hour.

The group started on their journey again the following evening. Eusebio was strangely refreshed and buoyant. They were headed toward a place called Dripping Springs. Eusebio looked forward to sleep, hoping for another dream. But the duchess did not appear to him that night, nor any other for many years.

After four days, they safely reached the other side of the desert passage and began looking for the Gila River. Eusebio was fifty-four; unlike his younger self, he now needed his rest. When he and Manje finally came to the edge of the river, they stopped to refresh their horses. They chose a pleasant spot, with only the sound of insects buzzing lazily in the warm air. The men stretched out on the dry, yellow grass. As Manje closed his eyes, Eusebio was mesmerized by the water flowing quietly past.

Silently and suddenly, one hundred Yuma men appeared, paddling long boats along the river. Eusebio sat up with a start and pushed Manje's shoulder to wake him. The Yuma pulled at their paddles to stop the boats at the sight of Eusebio and Manje, who immediately realized they had somehow entered Yuma territory.

The Yuma men expertly maneuvered their boats to the grassy bank. They emerged from them tall and broad-shouldered, towering over Eusebio and Manje, who instinctively jumped up and backed away in fear. The Yuma men smiled and spoke a few words in greeting. Eusebio replied in the Pima language, explaining that he was friendly and that he was a priest.

The Yuma cacique among the group—Eusebio recognized the feathers in his hair as a sign of leadership—stepped forward to present a gift. Eusebio's eyes widened—it was a blue abalone shell, exactly like he'd seen on the western coast of Baja years ago. He wished he could ask the cacique where the shell had come from. Instead, he nodded and thanked him.

He still carried the one given to him by the native woman that night on the coast of Baja, California. She had obviously picked it up on the shores of the Pacific Ocean. Later, when he and Manje were far away from the friendly Yumas, he pulled out both blue shells—they were identical. Possibly traded many times before it reached his hand, this one must have come from the same place—but how and by what route? He must find that route.

The next morning, waking early and feeling restless, Manje rode his horse alone into the nearby mountains. There he saw a view that filled him with excitement—he couldn't wait to tell Eusebio. In the distance, the two great rivers, the Gila and the Colorado, clearly joined.

But they would have to explore these magnificent rivers another time. Supplies had run dangerously low and they'd lost several horses after the desert trek. They had to return to Mission Dolores.

The shells had revived Eusebio's obsession with Baja—could he prove it was a peninsula and not an island? To do so was beyond his missionary duties, and he was not sure he could gain approval from his superiors to spend time away from his missions.

When he and Manje returned to Mission Dolores, Eusebio called a Blue Shell Conference and invited chiefs from many tribes. He sent a messenger to the east to invite Chief Humari and his son. He sent another north to inquire after the chiefs of near Spanish settlements of Le Encarnación, San Andrés, and Santa Catalina. He invited chiefs of the Coco Maricopa and the Yuma, and chiefs of the Pima. It was always good to extend hospitality to these chiefs, but Eusebio had a particular purpose this time: he wanted their knowledge of the source of the blue shells and the best route to Baja.

On the appointed day, the caciques arrived. When they were finally assembled, Eusebio invited them to sit in a circle, as was their custom for important meetings. He began with a prayer and a blessing for them all. Then he placed the two blue abalone shells on the ground before them.

"Where do these come from?" Eusebio asked. "The gulf?"

"No," Chief Humari said. The chiefs were all in agreement. "These shells are not found on the gulf—only the far side of Baja."

Eusebio asked how far away Baja was. A journey of ten or

twelve days, at least, the chiefs replied. They gave their accounts of the best routes.

That night, Eusebio wrote to Padre González, telling him of this meeting. He stated his intention to find his way by land to Baja from Mission Dolores. When he finally received Padre González's response, it filled him with joy and relief:

If Your Reverence accomplishes the entry by land into Baja, we shall celebrate with great applause, whereby the world will be enlightened as to whether it is an island or a peninsula, which to this day is unknown. I greatly desire that Your Reverence may finally make this most desired expedition by land into Baja. If you accomplish this, we must erect to you a costly and famous statue. And if the way is short, there will be two statues. May God give Your Reverence health and strength for this and many other equally good things.

Eusebio held the letter for a long time. He certainly would not agree to a statue of himself. But statues that would have meaning long after his time would be one of Jesus and the other of Our Lady of Sorrows.

"Two hundred and eighty," Eusebio wrote in his diary. It was September 1700, and he and ten Spanish servants with horses and mules had set out on a new northward expedition. They had just entered a settlement called San Gerónimo, an area populated with natives who grew fields of maize and pumpkins.

CHAPTER TWELVE

The white men had been greeted warmly by exactly 280 men, women, and children.

"Upon inquiry, we learned that in this vicinity, into which we had never before entered, there were more than a thousand persons who had never before seen a father or any Spaniards," he wrote. Here he baptized three adults who were ill and seven babies.

Days later, he and his group reached the Gila River. With the help of Yuma guides, they headed west to the head of the Gulf of California. He began looking for a high point from which to see whether Baja was connected to the rest of New Spain. He had brought with him a fine telescope. The clear day gave him an unimpeded view, and now he could see it clearly, though far off in the distance.

"Looking and sighting toward the south, the west, and the southwest, both with and without a long-range telescope, we saw more than thirty leagues of level country without any sea, and the junction of the Río Colorado with Río Gila and their many groves and plains," he wrote. Eusebio questioned his guides, and they easily confirmed what he had seen—Baja was indeed connected to New Spain.

That night, as he pulled out his maps to make adjustments, his Yuma guides interrupted him with a pressing request. Their chief wanted to see Eusebio. Naturally, Eusebio agreed, and as he followed the men the next day, he marveled how his work as a missionary and a cartographer were so intertwined. The explorations brought him close to the Yuma people, so he was able to talk to them about God. And they showed him routes through this rough country, so that his maps became increasingly accurate. He thanked God.

They marched back to the Gila, then to the Colorado, where they were met with a dramatic sight: the Yuma chief and one thousand people of the tribe had come to greet Eusebio.

Communicating in Pima languages they both shared, Eusebio warmly acknowledged the chief. The chief invited Eusebio and Manje to sit in a circle with him, as well as a young Spanish servant who was able to translate. The chief wanted to discuss God and the Christian faith, a subject that fascinated many of the Yuma.

Eusebio settled in for a long talk, and he was surprised and delighted—though he could not understand all they were saying, it was clear they wanted to know about his religion and offer their opinions and experiences. The chief asked a question about the Christian god. Eusebio leaned in closely, trying to get his meaning.

"He's asking if Jesus is a spirit guide," the translator said.

"Spirit guide? No, I think my spirit guides are my fellow Jesuits," Euesbio said, though he was not sure what the term *spirit guide* meant. "Jesus is my savior. He died for me, for all of us."

Once this comment was translated, the chief and his companions looked confused. "Why did he die?" they asked.

"He was betrayed, but it was a fulfillment of a prophecy. He was murdered—crucified on a cross—for our sake." The chief and his men received this information with concern. Eusebio realized how confusing this story sounded. "But Jesus rose again after three days, and he lives with God."

The chief smiled as he finally understood. "Like Coyote—he can't ever be trapped. He's too intelligent," he said. Eusebio nodded and smiled at this interpretation and decided no other was needed.

"These talks—ours and theirs—lasted almost the whole afternoon," Eusebio wrote in his diary that night, "and afterward until midnight, with great pleasure to all."

As soon as he returned to Mission Dolores, Eusebio reported to his Jesuit superiors in Mexico City that Baja was confirmed a peninsula, and that he had met with the Yuma. He received letters of praise and congratulations from them, as well as from Spanish officers who admired his accomplishment. This new geographical understanding would help the ambitions of both the missionaries and the army.

His old friend and fellow Italian, Juan Salvatierra, had already traveled to Baja; he settled in areas where Eusebio and Admiral Atondo had lived years before.

The two Italian priests wrote to each other often. Salvatierra described his new settlements and pleaded for Eusebio to send as many sheep, goats, and cattle as he could for the burgeoning missions. "It has cost sweat, blood, and great treasure," Salvatierra wrote, "but through the patronage of Most Holy Mary, the gospel is being spread from sea to sea."

Eusebio immediately set about organizing large numbers of cattle to be sent from mission ranches to Baja, either by land or boat. Cattle were critical. Not only were they raised and killed for food, but their fat was used for tallow, an essential ingredient for soap, candles, and cooking.

Then Salvatierra sent him a new letter with an exciting idea. He would sail across the gulf and meet with Eusebio, and the two could return to Baja by land, forging the first route for Spaniards from New Spain to the Baja Peninsula. Eusebio agreed and invited his longtime traveling friend, Lieutenant Manje, to join them.

On a cool spring morning in April 1701, Eusebio was in a deep sleep, as usual, under a tree next to Mission Dolores. He had developed a fever, and now he twitched—and even laughed—in his sleep. A young girl passing by with a water jug on her head glanced at the slumbering priest and hurried away from him.

Eusebio slept through his fever. His ambitious expedition with Padre Salvatierra and Lieutenant Manje was over, and his body was weak and tired. Their goal had been to trek the entire distance from Mission Dolores to the settlements Salvatierra had founded on Baja.

They had been convinced of their success. Eusebio had brought his maps and astrolabe and marked each point accurately. They had happily set out together in early 1701, the hired servants laughing as the priests sang songs on the trail. But their good mood evaporated when, after many hours, they could not find water. More than once, they feared they might die of thirst.

The pack animals, already weakened by hunger and thirst,

stumbled dangerously over rocks and boulders. Some fell and broke limbs. Nearing Yuma territory, some guides refused to go on, claiming Yuma had fallen deathly ill from a sickness they got from the Spanish.

The goal of reaching Baja by land finally had to be abandoned—for now. But all three men had climbed a mountain peak and were rewarded with a view of the gulf, and of Baja curving up to connect with Mexico.

Here they made a promise: they would try again as soon as possible to establish a viable land route to Baja, and with better preparation and more supplies. Then they went their separate ways.

The duchess listened to all this attentively, once again visiting Eusebio in his dreams. This time, she appeared out of the plains and sat next to the tree where Eusebio tossed and turned in his feverish sleep. As he told her of these recent exploits, he noticed how eagerly she took in each word. The passage would always be there, she assured him, to explore when he was ready.

"And all along the way, we baptized children and adults, and sat with caciques, talking and gesturing like old friends," Eusebio said. Only when he spoke to the duchess would he let himself express pride in his accomplishments.

"Don't forget that the missions you started here need your attention," she reminded him. "These Christian outposts must endure for years to come. Build them up, make them strong."

"Yes, yes. You are right," Eusebio replied in his dream. The duchess reached out and placed her cool hand on his burning forehead.

Chapter Thirteen

ATTACK ON MISSION DOLORES

For the next two years, he did as he promised the duchess in his dream. Eusebio spent months at each of his missions in the Pimería Alta. He organized men to help him expand the buildings. He planted more fields and dug more irrigation ditches. He built sturdy fences so each mission could keep more cattle. He welcomed new young missionaries and helped them settle. He nurtured the mission vineyards—the Spanish colonists had proved to be steady customers for the wine made by the Jesuits.

Now, as he rode back to Mission Dolores after a month away, his mind reviewed his worries: Apache warriors were a constant threat, causing his Pima friends to live in fear. Silver that Eusebio bought and sent to Spain never reached its destination. Somewhere along the route, those gifts he intended for the Jesuits in Cádiz were lost forever. And news was spreading that certain Spanish military officers wanted to put the Jesuit missionaries in their place—that claims of land were theirs to decide, not the indigenous peoples'.

Eusebio prayed for God's protection. He didn't like to admit it, but he was discouraged. So often he was a lone crusader for justice. Spanish officers again and again intruded on lands Pima tribes had inhabited for years—and killed them when there was a hint of resistance.

He straightened up abruptly in his saddle. As he approached Mission Dolores, he could tell there was trouble. A fence he'd built was smashed and cattle were roaming across the nearby field of crops. Eusebio urged his horse forward, then he jumped off to run into the mission residence.

It was empty. Not one of his Pima friends or hired workers could be found. Doors were left wide open; inside, chairs and tables were pushed over. Pots and dishes lay strewn across the floor, broken in pieces. Eusebio ran outside and shouted out, but no answer came.

"Padre," a little voice finally called to him. He spun around to see a little Pima boy creep out from behind a bush. "Padre!" The boy ran to him. Eusebio knelt down and looked into the boy's tear-streaked face.

"What has happened, my son?" he asked gently in the boy's language.

"They came and took everyone! I was hiding and they didn't find me," the boy said, choking. Eusebio hugged him.

"Who took everyone? Who came here and did this?"

"Spanish men, the ones with guns," the boy said. "They took my mother and my father." He began to cry again.

Eusebio brought the boy to his horse and helped him up. He mounted, and the two rode off to the nearest Pima settlement. He would make sure the boy was safe, then find out who had done this.

"They say your Pima at Mission Dolores were working there against their will."

Eusebio stood in an office in Guadalajara before a military official who laid out the accusations against him. "And our man—I will not tell you his name, Padre—claims he freed them from your enslavement."

"That is nonsense and you know it," Eusebio said. "Where are they? I will easily find out the name of the officer who did this. He had no right to kidnap people from my mission!"

"Hold on, he says they were there against their will—"

"You know I would not do that." Eusebio eyed the officer, who smirked. *So, they will spread lies about me so they can do what they want*, he thought. "Right now, you must tell me where he has taken the people he kidnapped. I have a small boy who wants to see his parents."

After studying Eusebio's wild hair and torn cassock with utter disdain, the officer finally named the ranch where the Pima had been taken. "It's too bad you like to make trouble, Padre," the officer said. "They will get much better care as slaves at that ranch."

"I pray for God to forgive you for these terrible deeds, and that one day you realize what you've done," Eusebio said.

It took him a month to find all the Pima people who'd

been kidnapped from Mission Dolores and return them to their communities. But his anger about the accusations pointed at him lingered. He made sure the administrator at the Spanish headquarters in Guadalajara recorded that the Pima had lived at Mission Dolores on their own free will, and that they were paid fairly for their work.

Clearly, certain Spanish officers wanted to damage Eusebio's reputation. It was September 1704 when Eusebio caught the rumor that the cacique of the Cocóspora was plotting a revolt, a massive attack against a Spanish settlement.

Eusebio knew this chief well. He was a friendly old man and gentle spirit who always brought baskets—woven with intricate patterns by the women of his village—filled with food each time he visited. It would be unlike him to plot a dangerous revolt, and Eusebio suspected some Spanish officer had started this rumor to justify an attack on this chief and his people.

He sent a messenger to the chief, alerting him to this dangerous possibility and urging him to come to an official hearing in Cucurpe. Not only did the chief come, but he brought his two grown sons. All three walked tall with regal bearing. They wore feathered and beaded necklaces. Eusebio greeted them solemnly and accompanied them into the building to meet the official investigator, and he smiled in surprise when they met him. He knew the investigator well—he attended Eusebio's mass every Sunday at Mission Dolores. The man was of limited intelligence but had great faith—he always brought his wife and small children, and even gave a small donation to the mission.

The investigator nodded at Eusebio with an uncomfortable smile. Eusebio greeted him and explained that the chief came to make an official report.

"All right, please tell the chief to begin," the Spanish investigator said.

The chief stepped forward to tell his story. He and his Pima tribes wanted to live in peace with their neighbors, he said. They had no intention of an attack and he was grateful for all Eusebio and the other missionaries had done for their settlement. The investigator listened without expression, dipping his pen into an inkwell and writing in neat letters the essence of the chief's declaration. He told Eusebio he would report these words to the Spanish officials.

The rumors stopped—for now. Eusebio could only wonder what next lie the Spanish would tell about him. He vowed to make sure he was alert and ready to take necessary steps to counter the falsehoods. He did not have to wait long.

Word came that the Spanish had accused another cacique of plotting attacks—this time against Jesuit missions. Eusebio wasted no time in riding his horse to find the chief. After explaining the rumors, Eusebio urged him to make a declaration of loyalty to the same Spanish official.

The chief did so, to Eusebio's great relief. He had again stopped a lie that would probably have led to the death of many innocent Pima people.

Chapter Fourteen

PROTECTING THE FLOCK

Four Italians had reached notable positions in New Spain. Padre Juan Salvatierra was now in charge of all the Jesuits of Mexico. Padre Francisco Píccolo was named visitor of the entire Sonora region, and Eusebio of course directed many missions in addition to Mission Dolores. Now a new missionary, Padre Gerónimo Minutuli, was headed to the mission at Tubutama centrally located north of Dolores.

The four men were all proud of their Italian upbringing, but they were unified by an even more important bond: as Jesuits, they shared the same approach to missionary work. They wholeheartedly supported the indigenous people and worked for years to improve the lives of all natives, bringing to them the wisdom and love of Christ.

"In spite of the devil, who seeks confusion, those apostolic missions are going to be founded and advanced," Padre Píccolo wrote to Eusebio, explaining his determination to help the missions succeed. "Have patience and fortitude, Your Reverence, for I trust in the Lord that all will be adjusted and composed."

When he was finally able to visit to Mission Dolores, Padre Píccolo was delighted by its vibrant and thriving community. Here was a large church with shining bells and ornaments, a solidly build residence, a flourishing garden, and a vineyard and winery, all run by Pima people who'd been trained and paid for their labors by the winery's income. Marveling at the fenced-in fields, which held healthy herds of horses, goats, sheep, and cattle, he praised Eusebio for all he had done.

Eusebio ignored the praise. *God is to be praised, not me*, he thought. A lot of work by many people spanning years created this productive place. And he knew Spanish ranchers were eager to snatch it all away if they could. He never took the current peace for granted.

With Padre Píccolo, he visited all the other missions he'd helped establish, impressing his superior at each stop. When the two men returned to Mission Dolores, Eusebio had an idea. "We must have a celebration for your visit, Padre," he said.

He knew a few things Píccolo didn't. The Pima took celebrations seriously. And the Spanish—the ranchers, as well as the army officers—would feel compelled to honor a respected priest. In his clever way, Eusebio once again set the scene for a peaceful meeting.

Padre Píccolo waved his hand in attempt to dismiss the suggestion, but Eusebio insisted. He sent messengers to tribal chiefs, missionaries, and Spanish ranchers, miners, and officials alike, inviting them to come in two days for a feast.

It was a joyous occasion that began with a procession, led by Eusebio holding aloft a shining silver cross, and ended with great bowls of fruits, grains, and wine set out for everyone to enjoy. The crowd mingled uneasily, but in deference to the Jesuit priests, they were outwardly respectful to one another.

Chapter Fifteen

A FINAL VISIT

M*y bones hurt.* This was Eusebio's first thought upon awaking these days, and today was no exception. He was sixty-one, yet still preferred sleeping on the ground. Once he stood up and stretched his legs, the aching pain went away. After strolling through Mission Dolores and breathing in the fresh, cool morning air, he was once again invigorated.

It was time for another expedition—this time to the islands located off the western coast of Mexico, just south of Acapulco. The sun's glow gilded the tops of trees. He was proud of all he'd done. His twenty-four missions were all self-sustaining through crops, cattle, and wineries. He'd kept meticulous notes about all the men, women, and children he had baptized on every expedition, and those numbers had grown. He knew the approximate populations of each village and settlement he visited.

But he was especially proud of the maps he had drawn, the first ever of these areas. He revised them each time he traveled and included new missions and settlements. He also indicated the names of tribes who inhabited each region—another first. He even sent one map to the duchess, asking her to pass it on to his Ingolstadt cartography teacher and friend, Father Heinrich Scherer.

But now it was time to investigate the location of these islands. He strode over to his adobe office building to write to his friends to see who might join him on this new expedition. He had barely begun his letter when he was interrupted by a visitor, a young Jesuit missionary who'd ridden all the way from Guadalajara. The man was visibly agitated.

"Good brother, what is the trouble?" Eusebio asked, inviting him to sit.

"Padre, I come with serious news, I'm afraid," the young priest replied.

"Out with it, then!" Eusebio was suddenly worried.

"It is your old friend Juan Manje. As you know, he has become a general. He has written a book with a disturbing point of view, saying our Jesuit missions have made it impossible for the Spanish ranchers to develop the land for themselves. He suggests lands be taken away and given to the Spanish."

Eusebio could not believe what he was hearing. What had happened to his old friend?

"There is more," the young priest continued uneasily. "He says that silver mining should be expanded, and that our native friends must be pressed into service for the hard labor."

Eusebio paced around the room, trying to absorb this news.

"Finally, he has said that Jesuit priests are so few and far between that they cannot serve our communities. They have even denied confession to Spanish soldiers."

"I don't understand what has changed his heart," Eusebio said. "How has this been received?"

"I'm sure you can imagine, not well. Manje was taken from his home and put in prison."

"Prison!"

"The governor asked him to produce a letter signed by witnesses who agree with his view or remain in jail. Manje chose jail, and there he stayed until he agreed to revise his book with a kinder view toward the Jesuits."

"Thank you for telling me," Eusebio said, sitting down heavily in his chair. Sensing Eusebio needed time alone, the young priest rose and left.

Eusebio remembered that Manje had come from a family of military men. He guessed that as Manje grew older, he had reunited with his uncle and other family members who were landowners. Perhaps he had his own ranch by now.

The situation had been dealt with by his superiors, and Eusebio felt no need to interject or even reach out to his old friend and traveling companion. But he was stung by the words he'd just heard. He had many memories of his adventures with Manje and had seen his friend demonstrate great kindness toward Pima people countless times. He resolved to keep his thoughts to himself, and if ever asked, he would only speak well of his former friend.

He was afraid that many Spanish officials and landowners shared Manje's logic, and that it was only a matter of time before they forced the Pima and other tribes off their land so they could take it as their own. He would do all he could to prevent it, with God's help.

After all these years, he knew many caciques and had learned their ways. He performed mass, sometimes out in the open on top of a rock, other times in one of the small mission chapels he helped build with his own hands. Even at his advancing age, Eusebio still drove herds of cattle, burros, sheep, and goats to far-off villages and missions that needed them. His dark hair had long ago turned gray, and dust seemed permanently absorbed into his leathery skin. Still, Eusebio exuded the calm of a man walking in God's grace, a man who has done what he hoped to do. He no longer believed he could save the world, but he still woke each day with the desire to try.

In the early months of 1711, he rode to the town of Magdalena to dedicate a new chapel to Francis Xavier, his personal patron. His good friend Padre Campos would be there—now forty-two, he had always revered Eusebio's determination.

Campos was astounded that Eusebio had established twenty-four missions in these barren lands. Eusebio still visited them to make sure they had what they needed to thrive, but more often lately he'd stayed at Mission Dolores to read the Bible under the trees or by candlelight, and to enjoy the bustle of work and the changing light of each day. For more than two decades, Eusebio had explored these deserts, mountains, and rivers. They were now more familiar to him than any other place. He was at peace just listening to the birds.

Now Eusebio moved slowly to the center of the small adobe

chapel. He stood and prayed next to a wooden table, upon which a simple silver cross had been placed. Before him, with heads bowed, a small group of people from several tribes had gathered to listen. After blessing them in their native language, Eusebio began to speak the familiar Latin words of mass.

Suddenly, his body felt weak. His rough hands shook and his knees buckled. He collapsed to the floor. Campos rushed to his side and cradled the older man's head in his hands.

As a cool breeze swept over Eusebio, he turned to see the duchess enter the chapel and sit by his side. She picked up his hand. "Now I know . . . you have been my spirit guide," Eusebio said with a weak smile. "Sent by Jesus to care for me."

"Yes," she said, looking into his eyes with the love of an old friend. "And you have done his work here. Now it's time to rest, to be with the Father."

Eusebio smiled. Campos carefully lifted Eusebio and carried him to bed. He sent a messenger to Mission Dolores with the urgent news: Come quickly—our Padre Kino is dying.

The response was swift. By the end of the day, hundreds of Pima people, many with children strapped to their backs, hurried on foot to the mission. Priests from other missions immediately set out for the location, arriving as soon as they could. In the early hours of March 15, 1711, Padre Eusebio Francisco Kino stopped breathing.

Pima who had come from nearby settlements were joined by nearly a thousand or more—people of other tribes who traveled great distances to say goodbye to the man who had given his life to improving theirs. Soldiers, ranchers, mine owners, and Spanish officers arrived too, taking off their hats as they approached the small adobe mission.

Eusebio was buried by Padre Campos next to the little chapel. In the cool shade of a huge cottonwood tree, people of all ages quietly gathered to watch as the rough wooden coffin holding Eusebio's body, wrapped in light cotton made by Pima women, was carried out and lowered into a hole.

Campos spread out his hands and blessed the crowd. The caciques spoke, remembering their friend and champion. Then they sang, looking up to the sky as if Eusebio were already among the clouds.

Beating their drums softly to celebrate Eusebio's passing to the spirit world, they danced solemnly. A dry gust of wind swirled sand up around them.

As Campos watched the ceremony with tears in his eyes, he made a vow. He would make sure no one would ever forget Padre Eusebio Kino and all he had done.

Sonnet

Praising The Astronomical Science Of
Father Eusebio Francisco Kino Of The Company Of Jesus,
Who Wrote About The Comet That Appeared In 1680,
Absolving It Of Evil Portent.

Although heaven's pure light is bright, bright
the moon and bright the stars, and bright are
the fleeting lightning flashes that are borne
by the air and sped by fire;

even though lightning is bright, its laborious
production costs the wind a thousand
discords, and the flash produced in its path is
a dreadful light in gloomy blackness;

all dull human knowledge is obscure without
mortal plumage being able to be,
with proud flight,

Icarian in rational discourses, until yours,
superb Eusebio, you brought light to the
celestial lights.

—Sor Juana Inés de la Cruz

Translated by Fred McAninch. The original Spanish sonnet can be found in *Sor Juana Ines de la Cruz, Obras Completas*, (Editorial Porrua, SA, 1972) 163.

About the Author

Nicole is a writer and editor living in Southern California with her husband and son. She has written for the *Boston Globe*, *Los Angeles* magazine, the *Los Angeles Times*, the *Orange County Register*, and other publications, and has edited a number of books. She particularly enjoys writing profiles of unknown people. In her free time she likes to travel, cook, and read fiction.

NOW AVAILABLE FROM THE MENTORIS PROJECT

America's Forgotten Founding Father
A Novel Based on the Life of Filippo Mazzei
by Rosanne Welch, PhD

A. P. Giannini—The People's Banker
A Biography by Francesca Valente

The Architect Who Changed Our World
A Novel Based on the Life of Andrea Palladio
by Pamela Winfrey

A Boxing Trainer's Journey
A Novel Based on the Life of Angelo Dundee
by Jonathan Brown

Breaking Barriers
A Novel Based on the Life of Laura Bassi
by Jule Selbo

Building Heaven's Ceiling
A Novel Based on the Life of Filippo Brunelleschi
by Joe Cline

Building Wealth
From Shoeshine Boy to Real Estate Magnate
by Robert Barbera

Building Wealth 101
How to Make Your Money Work For You
by Robert Barbera

Character is What Counts
A Novel Based on the Life of Vince Lombardi
by Jonathan Brown

Christopher Columbus: His Life and Discoveries
by Mario Di Giovanni

Dark Labyrinth
A Novel Based on the Life of Galileo Galilei
by Peter David Myers

Defying Danger
A Novel Based on the Life of Father Matteo Ricci
by Nicole Gregory

The Divine Proportions of Luca Pacioli
A Novel Based on the Life of Luca Pacioli
by W. A. W. Parker

Dreams of Discovery
A Novel Based on the Life of the Explorer John Cabot
by Jule Selbo

Humble Servant of Truth
A Novel Based on the Life of Thomas Aquinas
by Margaret O'Reilly

Leonardo's Secret
A Novel Based on the Life of Leonardo da Vinci
by Peter David Myers

Little by Little We Won
A Novel Based on the Life of Angela Bambace
by Peg A. Lamphier, PhD

The Making of a Prince
A Novel Based on the Life of Niccolò Machiavelli
by Maurizio Marmorstein

A Man of Action Saving Liberty
A Novel Based on the Life of Giuseppe Garibaldi
by Rosanne Welch, PhD

Marconi and His Muses
A Novel Based on the Life of Guglielmo Marconi
by Pamela Winfrey

No Person Above the Law
A Novel Based on the Life of Judge John J. Sirica
by Cynthia Cooper

Relentless Visionary: Alessandro Volta
by Michael Berick

Ride Into the Sun
A Novel Based on the Life of Scipio Africanus
by Patric Verrone

Rita Levi-Montalcini—Pioneer & Ambassador of Science
by Francesca Valente

Saving the Republic
A Novel Based on the Life of Marcus Cicero
by Eric D. Martin

Sinner, Servant, Saint
A Novel Based on the Life of St. Francis of Assisi
by Margaret O'Reilly

Soldier, Diplomat, Archaeologist
A Novel Based on the Bold Life of Louis Palma di Cesnola
by Peg A. Lamphier, PhD

The Soul of a Child
A Novel Based on the Life of Maria Montessori
by Kate Fuglei

What a Woman Can Do
A Novel Based on the Life of Artemisia Gentileschi
by Peg A. Lamphier, PhD

FUTURE TITLES FROM THE MENTORIS PROJECT

Novels Based on the Lives of:

Amerigo Vespucci
Andrea Doria
Antonin Scalia
Antonio Meucci
Buzzie Bavasi
Cesare Beccaria
Federico Fellini
Guido d'Arezzo
Harry Warren
Leonardo Fibonacci
Maria Gaetana Agnesi
Peter Rodino
Pietro Belluschi
Saint Augustine of Hippo

For more information on these titles and
the Mentoris Project, please visit
www.mentorisproject.org

Made in the USA
Las Vegas, NV
02 March 2023

68399689R00114